Dear Reader,

It is a privilege to be part of such a fine team of authors working together to bring you Miracles of Marble Cove. I loved spending time with Diane, Shelley, Margaret, and Beverly—the main characters in the books. Since mine is the fifth book in the series, I was able to read what the authors before me had written and was immediately captivated by the characters and setting of these wonderful stories.

Some might be wondering, *Why would a man enjoy spending time with and writing about a growing friendship among four women?* I happen to belong to a peculiar group of guys who enjoy watching romantic comedies, Jane Austen movies, and anything on the Hallmark Channel or *Masterpiece Theatre*. My wife, Cindi, has always been my best friend. I love listening to her thoughts and ideas about life.

Although we've never actually been to Maine, part of my childhood was spent in New England. I have a friend who spends much of her time there each year. She sent me a treasure trove of pictures, stories, and Web sites to explore about Maine's coastal towns and lighthouses. It made the town of Marble Cove come alive for me. And now Cindi and I are committed to getting up to Maine as soon as we can.

I hope you enjoy reading *Autumn Light*. The story revolves mostly around Diane, but her three friends experience some significant challenges and new opportunities as well. And, of course, new secrets are always waiting to be explored at Orlean Point Light.

Blessings,
Dan Walsh

Autumn Light

MIRACLES *of*
MARBLE COVE

Autumn Light

DAN WALSH

New York, New York

Published by Guideposts
16 E. 34th St.
New York, NY 10016
Guideposts.org

Acknowledgments

Every attempt has been made to credit the sources of copyrighted material used in this book. If any such acknowledgment has been inadvertently omitted or miscredited, receipt of such information would be appreciated.

"From the Guideposts Archive" originally appeared as "A New Leaf" by Diana M. Amadeo in *Guideposts* magazine. Copyright © 2006 by Guideposts. All rights reserved.

Cover and interior design by Müllerhaus
Cover art by Jeremy Charles Photography
Typeset by Aptara

Printed and bound in the United States of America
10 9 8 7 6 5 4 3 2

CHAPTER ONE

S tanding on the beach, just a few yards from where the promenade deck came closest to the sand, Diane Spencer closed her eyes and took a deep breath. Marble Cove had the freshest-smelling air on God's good earth. The rush of crashing waves filled her ears, and she couldn't help but smile. She opened her eyes again and noticed that the sky shone with autumn light. Fall was in the air.

It was the day after Labor Day. It should prove to be a very big day, Diane thought.

She knew Shelley, Margaret, and Beverly would be just as excited. She looked up at the Orlean Point lighthouse. She was supposed to meet them fifteen minutes ago but was running late. *They're probably already there,* she thought. In just a few moments, they would all be inside the lighthouse. But this time they wouldn't be coming through the front door. Today, they'd get in through the *secret* door, the one they had discovered in the lighthouse foundation a few nights ago, after her surprise party.

As Diane climbed a narrow pathway through the rocks, she heard voices on the other side of the lighthouse.

"Ladies, we've got to do this now. I can't wait here all day."
It was Detective Little. He was the reason the friends had had
to wait until after the Labor Day weekend to come back.

"Can't we wait a few more minutes, Detective?" Shelley
Bauer's voice rose over the surf. "Diane just called. She'll
be here any moment. We can't go in without her." Shelley
was the reason Detective Little had gotten involved in the
first place. The rest of the women had all been set to return
the previous Saturday with tools to pry open the secret door
themselves. Shelley, however, had had serious misgivings
about what Detective Little's reaction would be if he found
out they had gone in unescorted. Would he consider it
trespassing?

"I'm here!" Diane dusted the sand off and walked around
the base of the lighthouse to the east side. As she cleared the
structure, she looked down a slight incline that led to the
foundation, and she saw Shelley, Margaret, Beverly, and
Detective Little. She also saw that new young policeman,
Officer Crawley, standing behind Detective Little.

"We told him you'd be here any minute," Margaret said.

"And here I am. Sorry I'm late."

"It's good to see you, Diane," Beverly said.

"Isn't this exciting?" Shelley asked.

Officer Crawley smiled and nodded at Diane.

"Hey, Diane." Detective Little was the last to greet her.
He held a crowbar in his right hand. "We're getting ready to
bust this door open." He turned to face it. "I can't believe I
let you all talk me into this."

"What's the harm, Fred?" Margaret asked.

Officer Crawley held pruning shears. A pile of brush lay off to the side. "Those were some gnarly old branches," he said. "It took some effort cutting through that biggest one."

"Yes," Margaret said, "they've been growing here quite a while."

"No wonder no one ever saw this door before," Shelley put in.

"Well, someone knew about it," Diane said. "Do you see all those paint chips on the ground, Fred?"

"I see 'em." He bent down to examine them. "They're definitely the same as the trim on this door. But all that proves is someone tried to get inside. It doesn't prove they succeeded."

"They had to have succeeded," Beverly said. "How else would we have seen the lights turning on inside?"

Detective Little looked at her but didn't answer. Facing the door again, he stood up. He wedged the edge of the crowbar between the door and the jamb, just above the knob. Then he paused. "I don't know about this."

"You don't think you can get it open?" Diane asked.

"No, I'm sure I can pry it open. It's made of wood, not stone. It's just that once I do, I'm going to have to hire a locksmith to come back here and replace the lock. Which means I'm going to have to get the city to pay for it, which means I'm going to have to do a bunch of paperwork. And worse, now that this secret door is exposed, I can't just leave it here unlocked when we're through. Anyone can come back here and get inside. You know how curious people are, especially kids. Look," he said, pointing.

Diane and the others looked toward the road where he pointed. A group of four boys had gathered by the edge to watch, standing beside their bikes.

"I should have figured that would happen," he said. "We need to call this off. We can come back when I can have a locksmith standing right here. You know those kids will be over here the minute we leave."

"You can't call this off, Fred," Margaret said. "Look how many days we had to wait to get you here."

"Well, Margaret, I'm afraid curiosity's going to have to take a backseat to public safety. Besides, I might be able to get the locksmith here later this afternoon. The guy I use usually gets right back with me."

"But I can't come back this afternoon," Shelley protested. "We're celebrating Emma's birthday at Dan's parents' house, and I have to make cupcakes!"

"Me neither," Beverly said. "Can't you get us in there now? Then afterward, you could post Officer Crawley by the door until the locksmith comes. He can make sure no one gets in."

"I can't have Officer Crawley standing around here all day on guard duty. He's got—"

"Detective Little?" It was Officer Crawley. "Sorry to interrupt you, sir, but can I have a word? I think I might have a solution to all this."

Detective Little looked at him, then walked away from the door. Officer Crawley followed. They stopped just out of earshot and began talking quietly.

"What do you think they're saying?" Shelley wondered.

"I have no idea," Diane said. "But if it gets us inside that door now, I'm all for it." She noticed Fred Little finally nod. The men walked back.

"Officer Crawley acquired a certain skill before we brought him on the force," Detective Little said, moving to the right side of the door. Diane thought she saw Officer Crawley's cheeks flush.

Crawley bent down in front of the knob. He pulled something out of his pocket and held it with both hands in front of the knob.

"What, is he going to pick the lock?" Margaret asked.

"That's right," Detective Little said.

"Isn't that against the law?" Diane said, smiling.

"Very funny," he replied. Officer Crawley paused and looked up at his boss. "You keep going," Detective Little told him. "I said it's okay. Better this than hiring the locksmith. If it works, we'll just lock it back up when we go."

Everyone stood in silence for several minutes as Officer Crawley worked intently. At last, Diane heard a strong clicking sound.

"There, that should do it." Officer Crawley stood up.

"Well," Detective Little said, "see if it opens."

"It'll open." Crawley turned the doorknob and pulled a little, and the door gave way, creaking on its hinges. "There you go." He stood back.

It was pitch black inside.

"Good job." Detective Little tossed his crowbar in the sand and lifted his flashlight. "You ladies wait here. Let Officer Crawley and me check it out."

"Don't be silly," Margaret said. "We're coming right behind you. It's not like you're going to run into any monsters."

Diane laughed. It was so exciting. Detective Little walked inside, followed by Officer Crawley, then the ladies, in single file.

Diane's first impression was that it looked more like a tunnel than a room. It was maybe thirty feet long, angling upward.

"Where's this thing go?" Margaret asked. "Can you see?"

"It looks like it goes nowhere," Detective Little said. "It just dead-ends up ahead."

"Do you think maybe it's just an old storage room, sir?" Officer Crawley said. "Look at all these shelves along the top half of this one wall. They run the whole length."

"Maybe."

Diane also noticed what looked like a workbench under the shelves, with more shelves below that. "This can't be just a storage room," she said. "There has to be a way into the lighthouse itself from here. How else could someone get inside?"

Detective Little stopped, which caused them all to stop. "Well, Diane, look for yourself." He shined the flashlight forward. "It's just a wall, a paneled wood wall."

"Fred, shine that light back up near the top again, would you?" Margaret pointed, and Detective Little pointed the light. "See that, just along the top below the ceiling? Looks like a seam to me."

It did to Diane too.

"You may be right, Margaret." Detective Little reached up and felt along the edge. "There's definitely a cut running along here." He traced it until it stopped. "It's hard to see because of the way the boards meet, but I think there's a seam running down the side too. Hold this." He handed Crawley the flashlight then traced his finger down the other side too. "It's got a seam on both sides. This may be the way in. I can't pull it toward me, though. There's nothing to grab. Here, everybody stand back."

As the four friends backed up, he began to push against it, but it didn't budge. He put some weight into it a few times. Finally, it gave way, and he almost fell forward. "Well, how about that?" he said. Muted light filtered into the tunnel from the other side.

"There had to be a door," Diane said. "I just knew it."

"This is how that man has been getting inside," Beverly said, "to turn on those lights we've been seeing."

Detective Little walked into the open room, everyone right behind him. As soon as they came out of the tunnel, Diane recognized the room. They were in a part of the lighthouse that they had explored the last time they were here. "Well, look at that," she said as Detective Little turned and closed the makeshift door over the opening. A number of shelves had been built onto it from top to bottom. When closed, it almost disappeared and became a part of the wall.

"You know what I think?" Detective Little asked as he opened the door again. "This is some kind of hidden room. That's why we didn't see it before. We weren't meant to."

"Look, sir, under that workbench." Officer Crawley walked back into the tunnel and bent down. "Old wooden crates. There's a whole bunch of them. They're all lined up on the floor under these shelves." He slid a few out and set them on the workbench.

"Bring those in here," the detective said. "Let me look at them."

As Crawley set them on a counter, Diane noticed faded writing on the crates, and also that they were caked with dust.

"Is that the word *Peaches*?" Detective Little asked. "I can't make out the first one. It's some kind of company name."

"It is," Margaret said. "And that other word is definitely *peaches*. These are just old peach crates."

"I don't know," Beverly said. "You don't see many peach orchards in Maine."

"No, you don't," Detective Little agreed.

"Which means these crates probably contained something else," Diane added. "They must have stored other things in this room."

"It looks that way," Detective Little said.

Diane thought a moment. "I wonder what."

"And who? Whatever they were doing," Beverly said, "they needed a secret way in and out of this place to do it."

"Well," Shelley said, "it proves someone has definitely been coming in here these past few months, right through this tunnel."

The women looked at Detective Little, waiting for his response. "Okay," he said, "I can buy into what you're saying. To a point. But you still can't prove it is happening, just that it could be. Why would anyone sneak into the lighthouse off and on just to turn on some lights? He's obviously not living here. There's nothing in here worth stealing. Why would someone do that?"

The women stood there, exchanging puzzled looks.

"I don't know," Diane said. "I guess we still have to figure out that part of the mystery."

"Mystery," Detective Little repeated. "I really don't think there's any mystery going on here. I wish you would just drop this thing."

"Drop it?" Margaret said. "After this?"

"After what?" He gestured. "There's nothing here."

"We can't drop it, Fred," she insisted. "But we really do appreciate you taking time out of your busy day to help us here. Really, we do. You and Officer Crawley."

The other three added their thanks.

"Officer Crawley and I need to get going. Which means you ladies do too."

★　　★　　★

After Detective Little and Officer Crawley left, the four friends went to lunch in town. They discussed the peach crates and the secret door and what it could all mean. None of them could figure out why someone would sneak in there just to turn lights on and off.

"I'll be the first to admit it," Margaret said over the last of her meal. "I'm a little disappointed. On the one hand, it was so exciting to make this new discovery about the secret tunnel room. But then...I guess I'd hoped we'd find something more. At least something significant enough to win over a skeptic like Fred Little."

They all agreed.

"Still," Shelley said, "it was a good day overall, don't you think?"

"A good day," Beverly agreed. "But I don't know that we're much closer to solving the mystery."

★   ★   ★

Later that afternoon, Diane came back to the beach with Rocky near Orlean Point. As soon as they arrived, Rocky ran off, chasing seagulls near the water's edge. He never caught them but never gave up trying. The sand felt cooler between her toes than it had only a week before.

As she walked, Diane thought about what Eric might think of this new development at the lighthouse. She'd love to hear his take on all this. She still missed him terribly, but at least the emotional ambushes that used to overwhelm her had subsided. Now she could recall fond memories of their times together. She could savor the sweetness without lapsing into depression.

"Thank You, Lord, for that." She knew it was God's healing touch that been helping her, not the mere passing of time. Still, if she dwelt on it too long...

Rocky came bounding back and dropped a small piece of driftwood at her feet.

"Rocky, you're such a good boy!" *And so good for me to have you around.* She threw the stick as far as she could and Rocky tore after it.

As he ran off, she recalled something else that had been so good for her—her Labor Day visit with her two children, Justin and Jessica. After the surprise party her friends had thrown for her at the Shearwater Gallery last week, Justin and Jessica had stayed through the holiday weekend.

With every step, her toes got more and more frigid. She had to get her feet off the cold sand. She walked back toward the promenade deck. "Rocky, come! It's time to go." It was amazing how quickly summer had disappeared.

Rocky walked beside her. His stomach and paws were covered in wet sand.

"You're going to need a bath when we get home." Diane climbed up to the walkway, relieved to be walking on wood.

She glanced back at the lighthouse, half-hoping to see a light appear. She knew what they had confirmed today meant that at least one part of the lighthouse mystery was man-made. But she was convinced something more was going on.

Something supernatural, something...miraculous. What else could explain all the people who'd been rescued from the water around the lighthouse just after the mysterious light had appeared?

She heard the familiar sound of her cell phone ringing. But by the time she'd pulled it out of her pocket, she'd missed the call. On the screen were two voice mails, both from Frieda Watley, her literary agent. There was also one text message from her. All three had come in the last thirty minutes. The sound of the surf was just too much for her phone's ringtone to compete with. She read the text first:

Diane, please call me ASAP. Urgent!

CHAPTER TWO

The following morning, Shelley Bauer got her two children, Aiden and Emma, settled on the couch in the living room watching a DVD so that she could check on Dan. Usually by now, he'd be out here with them, eating his breakfast. Shelley had gotten up an hour earlier with the kids, so she and Dan hadn't talked yet this morning. She thought she remembered him saying yesterday that he had a full day of work down at the docks today.

As she walked down the hall, she worried he might have fallen back to sleep. The last thing they needed was for him to get in to work late and give the company a reason to let him go for good.

She walked into their bedroom, but the bed was empty. The only other place he could be was the bathroom, but she didn't hear the shower running. She walked over and found the bathroom door closed. It usually didn't take Dan more than a few minutes in front of the mirror to feel he was ready to face the day. Putting her ear up to the door, she heard some sounds in there, but what she thought she heard couldn't be right.

It sounded like Dan was crying.

She knocked gently. "Dan, is that you?" Well, of course it was, she thought. "Are you okay?"

The sounds stopped.

"Dan?"

"I'm okay. I'll be out in a minute."

He wasn't doing a great job hiding the emotion in his voice. That was not something she was used to hearing from him. "Honey, can I come in? It sounds like you're not doing too well."

"No, really, Shelley. I'll be fine."

"I'm coming in, Dan." She turned the knob, glad to find it wasn't locked.

He was standing in front of the mirror. He had just turned the water on in the sink and was wiping his face with a towel.

"What's wrong, Dan?" When she thought of the pressures they were both under these days, she realized it could be any one of a dozen things.

"I'll be okay," he said. "I guess it's just the stress. I wake up every day, and there it is. I feel so tired."

"Come here." She took his hand and led him out of the bathroom. "Let's talk."

"That'll just make it worse, Shelley. I'm trying to get my mind off of everything."

"It won't make it worse. Talking helps." She sat down on the bed. "Now you sit in the chair and talk to me. What's bothering you?"

"What about the kids?"

"The kids will be fine for a few minutes. They're all fed and cleaned up. They're watching a *Blue's Clues* video. Now talk to me. Is it the job? Almost getting arrested? The kids? Is it something I've done?" She figured if she primed the pump with enough topics, he'd start opening up on at least one.

"It's the job, I guess. Mainly. That and that stupid smuggling thing I got sucked into." He looked down. "I guess I'm just so tired of always being on the verge of going under. Nothing I do works out. I can't find a way to close the gaps."

She smiled sadly. "I feel it too."

"Like today…I'm getting dressed to head into work, but for what? I don't even know if there'll be enough work to finish out the day. Or if enough work will come in to get a full day tomorrow. The only thing I know we'll have enough of is bills. Those, I can count on every day."

She reached for his hand.

He released a pent-up sigh. "At least I still have you," he said. "And the kids."

Shelley brushed a strand of hair from his forehead. "There's something we could start to do," she said. "Something I know that would definitely help me."

"What is it?"

"We could pray together, at least every now and then."

He froze for a minute, then sighed again and nodded. "Okay, but… Maybe you'd better do it. You know I'm not good at that kind of thing."

Shelley bowed her head and led them in a quick prayer.

$\star \quad \star \quad \star$

After Dan headed off to work, Shelley took the kids to the playground. Emma, her youngest, sat happily in the stroller sucking her pacifier, while her three-year-old brother Aiden walked in small circles around them. Except for the times he stopped to study a bug or pull the petals off a flower.

"Mommy, Prize wanted to come with us to the playground," Aiden said. "I know what she wants. How come she couldn't come?" Prize was the puppy her husband Dan had brought home back in June.

Shelley laughed. "So you know what Prize wants, do you?"

"Yes. She jumps up and down and barks when she wants something. I asked her if she wanted to come with us. Know what she did?"

"Jumped up and down and barked?" she said.

Aiden nodded. "Why couldn't she come?"

"The city doesn't allow dogs to play in the park, honey."

"*Oooooh*," Emma said, through her pacifier. She pointed at a cluster of lavender lupines that had sprung up just off the sidewalk.

"That's pretty, Emma. *Pri-i-i-ty*." Shelley smiled. She loved seeing the little things in life through Emma's eyes.

Shelley pushed the stroller up a slight hill. The playground was just beyond it. She had decided to bring the kids there, hoping they might burn off some energy to give her and

Dan a quiet evening. That would be nice after the emotional morning they'd just had, and he'd be tired coming home from work. They'd given him a full day's work today, which was more than what he'd been getting lately.

"Why you shaking your head no, Mommy?"

"What?" Shelley looked down at Aiden, who was walking beside her.

"You're doing this." He shook his head back and forth.

"Mommy was just thinking."

"You were thinking of saying no? But I haven't even asked you yet."

She laughed. "What did you want to ask me?"

"When we get to the playground, can I go on the slide first?"

"Of course you can. As many times as you want. But you have to take turns with the other kids. Lots of kids like to play on the slide." She was glad school had started back up. That meant no big-kid bullies to worry about.

"Can Emma go on the slide too?"

"No, she's way too little. But I'm glad you asked. It's nice you want to play with your little sister."

"She doesn't have any fun toys. She can't do anything fun outside either. I'm glad I'm not little anymore."

Shelley smiled. She was *so* glad he still was.

What she needed to focus on now were the positive things God was doing in their lives. Today, Dan had work. The kids were both healthy. They lived in a lovely town. They were heading to a playground to have some fun. So much to be thankful for.

Shelley's thoughts were interrupted by something she saw as she crested the hill and the playground came into view: Madeleine Bancroft, sitting on a park bench. *"Friends call me Maddie."* Shelley heard Maddie's perpetually perky voice ringing in her head.

She seemed more like a Madeleine to Shelley. Madeleine Bancroft, Mrs. Perfect.

"Yay," Aiden shouted, as he saw the playground. "Time to play."

Yes, thought Shelley. Time to play.

Lord, give me strength.

"Oh, Shelley, hi! Come over here and sit by me."

Shelley waved politely. "It's okay, Aiden. You can go play on the slide. But stay right around here where I can see you."

"Okay, Mommy." Off he went.

Shelley looked at Maddie and smiled. Maddie Bancroft was about Shelley's age. But unlike Shelley, Maddie was perfect. The perfect wife, the perfect mother. She had four perfect kids, two the same age as Aiden and Emma, and two who were older. Shelley glanced around and saw three of them weaving in and out of the playground apparatus. Maddie's youngest, a little boy, sat beside her in a stroller.

Whenever Shelley got around Maddie, she had the feeling she was back in high school and Maddie, the head cheerleader, had just snubbed her because she didn't make the squad. When she first met Maddie a few years ago, her dark hair had been long and wavy. Now she kept it short, but it still looked...perfect. Even after four kids, she had the face and figure of a beautiful, much younger, woman. Maddie had invited Shelley over to her enormous two-story, four-bedroom home in one of the new subdivisions on the edge of town. Shelley had gone once. It made Shelley feel too inadequate to ever go back.

As expected, Maddie kept a perfect house.

"Sit down, Shelley. I just found out some exciting news. I'm dying to tell someone. I keep calling Roger, but I just get his voice mail. Oh my, look at Aiden. He's getting so big. Not as big as Roger Jr. was at that age, but he might be close."

As Shelley sat down, she looked over at Roger Jr. on the tire swing. Roger, Maddie's oldest, was eight. A few yards away, swinging back and forth on a squeaky blue horsey, was Katelyn, who was five. They weren't in school with the rest of the children in Marble Cove, because somehow in the midst of everything else Maddie did, she found time to homeschool them.

"So what's your exciting news?" Shelley asked.

"Well, the mayor called me just after lunch and said the town council wanted me to be the chairwoman for Marble Cove's fall fair. Isn't that wonderful?"

"*Hmm*," Shelley said. "I'm so happy for you. Isn't that a lot of work?"

"Oh, I'm sure it is, but it will be so much fun."

"The fair's at the end of this month," Shelley said. "It seems a little late to be picking the chairperson for such a big event."

"It is. The woman they had asked two months ago had to drop out at the last minute. But the mayor said she knew if anyone could pull it off, I could. Besides, most of the events repeat every year, and the people involved already know what they're supposed to do. As always, they'll block off the traffic on Main Street the whole weekend. All the stores and restaurants will set tables out on the sidewalk. The mayor said someone on the town council was going to notify them all this afternoon. Most of the restaurants use this event, you know, to showcase new menu items for the fall."

Shelley wondered if her friend Margaret planned to do anything at the fair. Her new art gallery was right on Main Street.

"And down the side streets," Maddie continued, "artists, crafters, and vendors will be setting up booths, giving lessons on how to make things, and selling this and that, like they do every year. Part of my job will be to coordinate all that. And of course we'll have the annual bake-off contest."

A table at the fair, Shelley thought, *and the bake-off contest...* An idea was beginning to form.

"Plus," Maddie added, "I've already cleared with the mayor two ideas I thought of last year. We're going to have horse-drawn carriage rides and face-painting for the kids."

"I'm sure they'll be happy about that," Shelley said. Emma started to fuss. Shelley pulled a little container of Cheerios from her diaper bag and gave her a small handful. She glanced over at Aiden, who was still on the slide. This had to be his tenth trip down by now.

"Oh, I almost forgot one," Maddie said. "And this is a biggie, something brand-new. I'm calling it the Chalk Walk

Contest. I'll have to run this by the town council, but I can't see them turning me down since the stuff washes right off. We'll let school-age kids from kindergarten through high school loose on the sidewalks in front of the library. We'll have three different age groups, and we'll give out trophies for each group. It'll be so much fun.

"Then on the last night I want to show *The Wizard of Oz* right up there on the back wall of the post office. It'll be just like the old days. You know, like a drive-in theater. Families can sit out there on blankets, eating popcorn and cotton candy in the grassy field. Won't that be something?"

Shelley nodded. It would be something, all right. But all she could think about was how Maddie could manage to do everything she did with that big house, homeschool her children, always manage to look stunning, and now manage a major citywide public event. Shelley was exhausted just hearing Maddie explain it all.

Lately, life itself exhausted Shelley. Just meeting the constant demands of her children, the housework, even the dog, wore her out. And now adding to the mix were her fears for their future. Would Dan's hours at work ever improve? Would they hand him a pink slip? They had almost nothing left in their savings account. How would they make it if that happened?

She and Maddie sat together on the bench for the next twenty minutes or so. Shelley only half-listened as Maddie rattled off her kids' significant achievements, one after the other. Aiden had finally moved away from the slide to explore other parts of the playground.

Shelley began thinking about the fall fair. What a perfect place to launch her new baking business. She'd get all kinds of free publicity. She could pass out samples right there on Main Street. The fair drew hundreds of locals and tourists each year. And wouldn't it be great if she could have her Web site up and running by then? Maybe she could have some brochures printed up that linked to the site. And maybe she could pick a recipe to enter into the bake-off contest. Winning that would draw all kinds of attention to her business.

"Isn't that wonderful?" she heard Maddie say, always the cheerleader.

"Yes, it is," Shelley said quickly and to avoid hearing her repeat it. She stood up and glanced at her watch. "It's been great talking to you, Maddie, but I have to go. Good luck with the fair." She pulled Emma's stroller onto the sidewalk. "C'mon, Aiden. It's time to head home." He whined a little, but she could tell he was tired. It was way past lunchtime, and he'd be more than ready for his nap afterward.

As she strolled down the hill, her newfound zeal began to crumble. All these ideas for the business...how could she pull them off? She was no Madeleine Bancroft. Who was she kidding? She wasn't the kind of person who accomplished great things. She could barely keep her household afloat.

No, she scolded herself, *don't go there*. She might not have all the brains, beauty, and talent of a Maddie Bancroft, but one thing Shelley did have...some great friends who'd be more than willing to help her.

Chapter Three

Margaret Hoskins added a tinge of gray to the bottom of a band of cumulus clouds. This painting for her new lighthouse series was coming together nicely. It was just after 3:00 PM. A CD player piped soothing jazz into the room. She'd just turned the sign over on the front door of the gallery, so that "Sorry, We're Closed" greeted anyone who came by.

She'd closed early today because she needed some undistracted time to paint. It didn't seem like a risky move, since hardly any customers had stopped by the gallery since lunchtime. That was just as well. It was hard to concentrate on her work when she kept getting interrupted by customers.

But, she reminded herself, they were the good guys. It was their patronage that allowed her to finally pursue her dream to paint and to actually open a gallery of her own.

However, judging from her sales records those first few months, she also knew that the customers who came in the gallery weren't enough to make ends meet. She sold some consignment paintings by other artists, which certainly helped, and she had sold a lot of her own paintings. But the truth was that most people who came in didn't buy anything. Still, it was satisfying to hear their reactions as they stopped in front of her paintings.

It was especially fun to hear them go on this way in her presence. Many assumed she just worked there. They'd ask about the artist, and she'd tell them who she was. She smiled as she thought about how fun those moments were: the look on their faces, the kind things they'd say. Who would have imagined living your dream at the ripe old age of sixty-seven?

Of course, encouraging words were nice, but they didn't pay the rent. She calculated that only about one in ten who walked into the store had actually bought a painting. Most said they'd wished they could but simply couldn't afford one. She felt bad, looking at their faces. It seemed as if they were begging with their eyes for her to lower her prices.

Well, she thought, as she dipped the tip of her brush again in the light shade of gray, she felt bad for *most* of them. One woman had come in that very day, just before lunch. A real snooty, bossy type. The woman had actually said, "If you'd lower the price of this painting to seventy-five dollars, I might buy it."

Margaret had looked at the woman's eighteen-carat gold Rolex watch and the shimmering diamonds woven into the wristband. Then she'd stared at the quarter-carat diamond earrings dangling from her ears. Not only could she afford to pay full price, she could probably buy all the rest of the paintings in Margaret's gallery.

Seventy-five dollars, Margaret thought. *Of all the nerve!* At that price, she'd be working for less than minimum wage.

She closed her eyes and took a deep breath, allowed Chet Baker's "Almost Blue," playing in the background, to calm her nerves. When she opened her eyes, she was staring at the painting in front of her. She loved it. She'd loved painting it, and she loved the memory it evoked from that day on the beach when this moment had captivated her imagination and she'd known she simply must capture it on canvas.

She loved the beach and was so thankful God had given her, Allan, and Adelaide the opportunity to move here to Marble Cove, where she could hear its sounds every day and see it whenever she wanted. She especially loved being able to swim in the ocean. She could actually picture herself swimming in this painting, just beyond the waves.

Now that summer had passed, she knew she couldn't swim much in the real ocean. The water temperature was always chilly, but it dropped considerably once the cold weather set in. But the painting before her would always be a beautiful summer's day in Maine.

She looked at her lighthouse, not all that different from the one on Orlean Point. In both lighthouses, the big light was turned off. But she'd imagined the lighthouse in her painting was still active. It made her ponder for a moment all the activity that had gone on over the summer at Orlean Point Light, which was supposedly an *inactive* lighthouse. Something exciting and mysterious was afoot; she was certain of it. She wished she had more time to pull on all the loose threads.

She looked back at her painting. It was her first new one under contract with Lighting the Way Greeting Card Company. They'd purchased a number of her recent paintings for a new line of cards, and now they had commissioned a new lighthouse series. Four paintings of the same location— one for each season of the year. It was also her first painting assignment that came with a deadline.

She wasn't sure she liked that part just yet.

On the one hand, this business relationship brought a sense of security. She had negotiated a generous contract with the greeting card company—certainly enough to take away her fears of closing down the gallery anytime soon. She'd been able to pay off all the repairs from that Fourth of July storm and had purchased all the paint and supplies needed to redecorate.

She swiveled in her stool and looked around, both here in the back studio and out into the gallery itself. She loved how everything had turned out in the remodel.

Allan's workload had picked up some in the last month, mostly from customers coming into the gallery, seeing his furniture pieces on display, and ordering some for themselves. He'd been keeping quite busy out there in his workshop. Of course, he was not working on a strict deadline. People would ask him how long it would take. Allan would tell them, "Four to six weeks, or thereabouts. But I'll make the wait worth your while." And they'd be fine with that.

Just then, Margaret heard the little bell ring in the gallery, the one above the front door. How could that be? She'd closed up almost an hour ago. She turned in time to hear the door open and close.

"Hello, anyone *he-yah*?"

It was a man's voice, an old voice. And clearly, a native Mainer. She stepped out from the studio and saw a white-haired man in a brown tweed suit standing just inside the doorway. He was looking at one of her paintings, the one on an easel closest to the counter.

"I'm sorry, sir," she said, "but the gallery is closed for the afternoon."

He looked up, and his face seemed familiar. She noticed a manila folder in his right hand.

"Oh, I'm sorry. I didn't realize."

She glanced toward the door. The sign still hung on its little suction cup and facing the right way. "Well, that's okay. Might have helped if I'd remembered to lock the door."

"Would you like me to come back tomorrow?" He pronounced it *ta-morrah*.

She knew she'd seen him around town but couldn't place his name. "No, that won't be necessary." She forced a smile. "You're here now, so how can I help you? Would you like to take a few moments to look around?"

"You have some lovely paintings here, that's for sure. And I know my wife would love this coffee table if she laid her eyes on it. But, no, I'm not here as a customer. The name's Bert Atwood, from the town council."

"Oh, Mr. Atwood. Now I recognize you. I voted for you, you know."

"Did ya now? Much appreciated."

If Margaret recalled correctly, Bert Atwood had been on the Marble Cove town council for decades. "So how can I help you, Mr. Atwood?"

"You might start by calling me Bert."

"Okay, Bert, what can I do for you?"

He set his manila folder on the counter and opened it. "You know about the Marble Cove's fall fair?"

"Yes, I love it. My husband and daughter and I go every year."

"Well, it's a-getting close, right around the bend. The end of this month, as a matter of fact."

"Is it time for the fair already?"

"Yep, end of the month. Think it's been the same time each year since just after we took over these parts from the British."

Margaret laughed, then realized it wasn't a joke.

He lifted a sheet from the folder. "Got a flyer here. Same one we use every year. For starters, it'd be a big help if we could tape this thing to your window. Let folks know it's coming."

"I'd be happy to do that, Bert. If you've got two, I could put one on the door and another in the window."

"Just got the one, I suppose. Got a lot of other stores still left on the street to see."

"I understand. One is fine."

He set it on the counter. "Have some tape in my pocket, if you need any."

"That's okay, Bert. I've got plenty."

"Do you plan on participating in the fair? I know your store is new since last year, so you might not be up to speed. But all the stores and restaurants on Main Street generally do sign up."

Margaret hadn't even given it a thought. "Why, yes. I want to do whatever is expected of me." She paused a moment. "Exactly what is expected, if you don't mind me asking?"

"Not at all," he said. "You don't have to close up shop for the weekend. Just move things out on the sidewalk, so to speak. You've been to the fair, so you know what happens. You'll be needing a table or two. Folks generally put a white tablecloth on them. Then you set out some of these here paintings you're selling, and folks come by to see them."

"Well, that shouldn't be too hard." She was sure Allan could help her set this up.

"Nothing to it," he said. "Of course, looking around your place here, you might get *all* your paintings out there on the sidewalk. Especially if you set up two tables." He looked around the gallery again. "Should all fit on two tables just fine. If you have any questions, you can call Madeleine Bancroft. She's heading things up this year. Know Maddie?"

"I've met her."

"Well, there you go. Someone wrote her cell number on the back of this flyer, real small there, down in the corner. Well, then, I best be moving on. Good day."

"Good day to you, Bert. Thanks for stopping by."

He walked out. Margaret waited a moment for him to get down the sidewalk a ways, then she locked the door. As she did, she released a pent-up sigh. That was just what she needed, another deadline.

She decided to put on a small pot of coffee and try to get her mind off this interruption. As she walked toward the coffeemaker, she stopped and looked around. Something Bert had said began to gnaw at her.

"Of course, looking around your place here, you might get all your paintings out there on the sidewalk."

It suddenly dawned on her what he meant.

She didn't have that many paintings left in the store to sell. She'd been so distracted by her new contract with the greeting card company, and they'd taken so many of her paintings, that she'd lost track of what had been happening in the gallery.

She might have a problem. A big one.

The fair was just three weeks away. It was entirely possible, if she kept the gallery open between now and then, that she might sell most or even all of her remaining paintings. She'd have very little left to display at the fair.

But she couldn't close the gallery down, not again. It had been closed for the better part of July for repairs after the storm. Business had begun to pick up because things had stabilized since then. Customers could count on the gallery having regular hours. Some of her customers would visit the store two or three times over the course of a week before buying their painting.

She could call the other artists, the ones who displayed their work here on consignment, to get them to bring in some more. But one of the things that bothered her was the ratio between her paintings and all the consignment works. So many of hers had sold over the summer that it was starting to feel less and less like *her* gallery. Still, that was only because she'd been so favored by the greeting card company, so this really was a nice problem to have.

She walked around, looked at her paintings again, thinking about which ones had taken the least amount of time to paint. She looked over at the computer on her desk. She'd made a habit of taking digital pictures of all of her paintings as soon as she'd finished them, including all the paintings she'd already sold. Maybe she could come up with a selection of the smaller ones to see if she could finish one each evening between now and the fair.

Was she kidding herself? She was barely staying on track with the new lighthouse series deadlines while trying to keep the gallery afloat. She'd never be able to get all those paintings done on top of what she was already doing.

She stood in front of her newest lighthouse painting and knew in that moment she was done for the day. She'd lost all her inspiration. She had to talk to someone, get some clarity in her head about how to solve this dilemma.

CHAPTER FOUR

Beverly Wheeland-Parker had just finished her run and was now cooling down in the side yard, doing a series of stretch routines before heading inside. She knew they looked odd done in public, at least here in Marble Cove. She often saw people out walking, but she rarely ran into other joggers. She'd endured a few too many stares when she'd done her stretching out front, so she'd begun taking advantage of the privacy offered in the side yard by the large stands of bayberry and viburnum that bordered the sidewalk there.

Mrs. Peabody, her elderly neighbor, had made such a face once upon seeing Beverly stretching that it had caused Beverly to instantly stop and apologize. Mrs. Peabody was actually very nice, but her ways seemed as old and dated as her lavender two-story Victorian home across the street. Beverly couldn't imagine ever seeing her in the prime of youth, out running in jogging sweats. And certainly not finishing up with these stretch routines. Heaven forbid.

Beverly imagined Mrs. Peabody much younger, strolling down the sidewalk on Newport Avenue in a billowing, flowery dress, spinning a parasol. Such attire was much more fitting for a young lady in public. She imagined her wearing the same outfit as she stood high atop the widow's walk at her house across the street, looking out toward the sea.

Beverly smiled as she stood up to go inside. Mrs. Peabody was old, but not *that* old. She had just stuck her back in the early 1900s. But she did have that air about her.

Stopping for a moment on the flagstone walkway, Beverly looked down the street at the neighborhood. She'd never lived here permanently before—her family had come to Marble Cove to stay only during the summers—but this really did feel like home. Not at all like the detached and lonely feel of that four-bedroom, three-bath house in Augusta she'd shared with her late husband, Will. As far as houses went, it was magnificent. It was the kind of house she had once dreamed about having. A real mark of success. But it was never a home.

Will had let her know early on that he intended to "wine and dine" prospective clients for his prestigious architectural firm there. It was why he'd designed and built it. And because of his emphasis on status and image, she'd been given an unlimited budget to furnish and decorate the place. Will had approved of her efforts. It was one of the few areas in their marriage where he'd actually volunteered some verbal encouragement.

But the exquisite house had barely kindled any feelings of home in the four years they had spent together, let alone the five years after his death when she'd lived there alone.

She was surprised at how easy it had been to drive away from that place. Oh, she still owned it—for now—and just yesterday she had contacted an agency to find renters to live there. But as far as she was concerned, she never needed to go back there to live. Until renters moved in, she'd use it when she came back into town off and on for business meetings over the next few months. She couldn't telecommute 100 percent just yet. It was just a house. A nice big house. It was a place she'd lived in for a few chapters of life, but they had been mostly unpleasant ones.

No, Beverly belonged here in Marble Cove. She was old enough to appreciate its value now and, at forty-two, hopefully young enough to make a new start. She looked around her father's home. Being here felt right.

A loud thump inside the house grabbed her attention. She rushed to the front door and flung it open. "Are you okay, Father?" She looked down the front hallway, which was lined with boxes she'd brought with her from Augusta. Another stack was piled up just inside the door in the living room.

"Huh? That you, Beverly?"

He sounded fine. "Where are you?"

He appeared on the far side of the boxes stacked in the hallway, a puzzled look on his face.

"Did you fall?"

"No," he said.

She noticed one of the boxes had fallen from the top row. Its contents had spilled onto the floor. Fortunately, it wasn't anything made of glass. Fearing the very scene confronting her now, she'd had the presence of mind over the weekend to ask Dan Bauer and Diane's son Justin—who had unloaded her things—to put all the boxes marked "Fragile" on the bottom row.

"I knocked one of these boxes over," her father said. "Not sure how, exactly."

She walked toward him. "Don't worry about it. There's no harm done. Are you hurt at all?"

"No, it didn't fall on me." He moved around the boxes and stood over the one that had fallen. She bent down and started repacking it, just a box full of kitchen towels and washcloths. "But I don't get how all these boxes got here in the first place," he said. "I thought I'd put them all up in the attic weeks ago."

Beverly sighed as she finished putting the last few dish towels in the box. She'd already told him where all these boxes had come from. And he'd been standing right there on Saturday when Dan and Justin had brought them inside from the U-Haul trailer out front. He'd even insisted he be allowed to help carry in some of the lighter ones.

It didn't anger her to have to keep reminding him, but it was beginning to cause her concern. His short-term memory loss seemed to be getting worse, even from just a few weeks ago. "Don't you remember? These are the boxes I brought with me from Augusta. I live here now, Father, remember?"

"Oh, that's right. I remember now. Need any help unloading the truck? I've still got some strength in these old arms."

"Thanks, Father, but we're all set. Remember, Dan and Justin were here Saturday, helping me move? You remember, Dan is Shelley's husband. Justin is Diane's son. They got them all inside."

"Of course I know Dan and Shelley!" He patted her cheek. "Do you need any help unpacking them then?"

"Not right now. Maybe in a little while. Can I get you anything? What have you been doing, reading your book?"

"Oh yes, my book."

Beverly set the box back on the stack and walked her father back toward his leather chair in the library. "You go have a seat and relax." She noticed his water glass was empty. He sat down, and she picked it up. "Let me refill this for you. Are you getting hungry? Do you want a little snack? Dinner's not going to be for a few hours."

"Maybe I could use a little something to eat."

"Would crackers and cheese be okay?"

"Whatever you think, dear." He picked his book back up and opened it to his bookmark.

She stood at the doorway of the library and looked behind him at the tall bookshelves filled with hundreds of books he'd read over the years. It had been his favorite pastime as long as she could remember. "As a teacher," he'd say, "I don't make enough money to travel, but my books let me travel all over the world, even to different places in time."

He was the main reason she'd come back home to Marble Cove. Since Will's death and her mother's death the following year, she'd been coming just on the weekends to look after him. Back then, the concern had been his blood sugar and whether he'd been eating properly all week. Now she worried whether he'd remember to eat at all. She had to get him to the doctor soon to see what this increased memory loss was about.

That reminded her that she also needed to get with Mrs. Peabody to let her know about the change in plans now that she was home to stay. At the end of June, she'd hired her to fix meals for her father during the week. Her granddaughter Belinda had also come over once a week to clean the house. That arrangement seemed to work well. Beverly dreaded having to tell Mrs. Peabody she no longer needed her help. She seemed to enjoy it and it seemed to give her such a sense of purpose. Plus, she knew Mrs. Peabody appreciated the extra income.

Maybe there was something Beverly could do to keep from shutting this arrangement down altogether. She walked past the boxes on her way back from the kitchen, her father's glass of water in hand. It would take so much work to get all of them unpacked and put away. Right now, she wasn't even sure where to put it all. And she needed to get the project done soon to keep her father from bumping into them every time he walked by.

Besides the unpacking, she had only the rest of this week off from work. She had discussed the possibility of permanent telecommuting with her new boss, Phil Miller, but he still insisted that she come back to Augusta for a number of important meetings they'd scheduled for the last quarter. She'd started to tell him about digital conferencing, how they could use cameras and the Internet to replace face-to-face meetings. But he was still feeling his way, and he knew she was very good in person. Halfway through that conversation, she knew she had been pushing him too far.

"I'll be back," she'd said, "whenever you need me to."

Between those trips back to Augusta and, starting next week, resuming her work here at the house, maybe she really did need Mrs. Peabody's help.

"Here you go, Father." She set the water, along with a plate of crackers and cheese, on the table beside him.

He looked up from his book. "Thank you, dear."

She smiled. "If you're okay here, I'll go check the mail. Then I need to take a shower."

"That's fine, Beverly." He smiled up at her. "It's so nice to have you here."

She opened the front door and walked out to the sidewalk. As she lowered the mailbox lid, a blue Toyota pickup drove by. It was Detective Fred Little, who lived next door. They exchanged waves and smiles. She wondered if his smile wasn't a tad insincere, thinking back to his cynical comments at the lighthouse yesterday. It was clear he thought they were becoming more of a nuisance, involving him in matters that were neither miraculous nor sinister.

Beverly wanted to believe miraculous things were taking place at Orlean Point, but something within her held her back. What if she fully embraced the idea only to learn they weren't miracles? She didn't know if she could handle the disappointment, so she didn't allow her heart to go there.

She kept her eyes on his truck, but Fred didn't pull into his driveway. He just kept driving by. At the end of the street, he turned right and drove out of sight. Was he avoiding her? No, that would be silly and immature. Fred Little was neither of those. She looked at her watch. It was too early for him to get off work. It was probably nothing. She should just mind her own business, get back in the house, and take that much-needed shower.

But seeing Fred reminded her of another reason she was glad to be back in Marble Cove. Beverly had turned up a number of new "lighthouse leads" last month in Augusta from her talks with Edward Maker. She was sure these new leads, coupled with their discovery of the secret room in the lighthouse, would turn up something exciting, maybe even solve the mystery altogether. Of course, looking into these things would take time, which was another good reason to keep Mrs. Peabody employed at the house.

Holding a thick bundle of bills and junk mail, she walked back into the house.

Her father stood in the hallway, opening the flaps to one of her boxes. Two others were on the floor beside him. He looked up at her. "Beverly. It's you. Now here's something peculiar. I got up to go to the bathroom, and look at this. Boxes everywhere. You know anything about this?"

"Actually, Father, I do. There's really a simple explanation. These are my boxes. I live here now."

"You do? How wonderful!"

CHAPTER FIVE

Diane had freshened up after her walk on the beach with Rocky, and now she sat on a comfy chair in the living room, sipping coffee, listening to soothing music, watching Rocky gnaw contentedly on a rawhide chew toy.

She, on the other hand, was anything but content.

Diane had picked up a new book to read, and this should have been the perfect moment to dive in. But all she could do was stare at her cell phone, waiting for her agent to call back. She was dying to know what was going on.

When she saw the text a little while ago on her porch, Diane had called her back right away. All she'd gotten was her voice mail. She'd listened to Frieda's two messages, hoping they might shed some light. She loved her new agent but hated the way she left voice mails. They were so brief, and she never gave any specifics. Didn't she know how tormenting that was? What was the harm in taking a few extra moments and spelling out the main thrust of your call, so you don't leave the other party dangling in suspense?

But her voice mails had offered no more information than her text had. *"Diane, please call me ASAP. Urgent!"* The second one had added this phrase: *"It's not really bad news."*

Had the people at the publishing house changed their minds? Were they pulling back from the deal? Diane had spent many years as a reporter, so she knew a thing or two about the publishing world. Which was why she was so shocked by several things that had happened after she'd finished the manuscript for her first novel.

First, it was a shock that she had gotten an agent so quickly. Most would-be novelists spent years trying to find an agent to represent them, piling up a drawerful of rejection letters in the process. She'd actually hesitated sharing her story with some newfound writing friends she'd met in a fiction group she'd joined on the Internet. Some had spent years "paying their dues" and had even written several books, yet still had not found representation.

And Diane had not secured just any agent, but Frieda Watley, from Brewster Literary Agency in New York City. A genuine A-lister. Frieda represented authors who'd won numerous national writing awards. Several were *New York Times* best sellers. It still excited Diane whenever she thought back to the moment she'd gotten that first call from Frieda.

She hoped Frieda didn't regret taking her on so soon.

The other amazing thing was how quickly Frieda had gotten a major publisher interested in her book. Judging by Frieda's enthusiasm and strong encouragement, Diane had allowed herself to think she might have actually written a decent book. She loved it, of course, because she'd written the kind of book she liked to read. But she also knew that writers tended to think too highly—and often inaccurately—about their own work. The real measure of a book's worth came from more objective assessments...like those of a reputable literary agent and publishing house.

"It's not really bad news." What did that mean?

Had the editor merely reacted so positively and quickly to her book because of Frieda's enthusiasm? Now that she had a little more time, had she decided to pass on it altogether? That would be horrible. Not just for Diane, but what about her friends in Marble Cove, who'd gone to so much trouble to give her that wonderful surprise party? And what about Justin and Jessica? They'd flown all that distance to be here for the party and had spent all that money.

There was another nagging concern, something Frieda had said in their earlier conversation about the book deal. Frieda had mentioned she'd found some problems in the contract. Or was it something she didn't agree with? She hoped Frieda hadn't pushed too hard and scared the publishing company off or made them mad. It didn't seem to Diane that she should push back at all. It wasn't as though Diane was in a strong bargaining position, like someone who'd already published a number of best-selling books.

Diane took a final sip from her coffee mug, looked at the cell phone screen again, then glanced down at Rocky. The happy expression on his face made her wish she had a rawhide chewy to munch on.

She put the book down. No sense pretending she was going to read it. She had to *do* something to get her mind engaged in a real activity. She thought about working on her second novel, but she knew that would just get her sucked back into wondering about Frieda's call.

Chop some onions and red peppers, she told herself. That was something. The dish she planned to make for dinner called for them, sautéed in olive oil. She stood up and had taken two steps toward the kitchen when her cell phone rang.

It was Frieda. "Hello?"

"Hey, Diane. Sorry I missed you. At a meeting with a publisher. Not yours. But had to shut the phone off, that kind of meeting."

"That's okay. I've just been sitting here, reading, listening to music, calm as could be."

Frieda laughed. "Yes, I could hear your calmness in your message. You poor thing. It's not bad news, really."

"Really? What's going on?"

"Okay, got a call from the acquisitions editor at—"

"Are they pulling out of the deal?"

"No, Diane. Nothing so drastic. You need to relax, take a deep breath. You've really written a good book here. That's why I said I'd represent you. I know I've told you that many times, but I guess I'll probably have to keep telling you that a hundred more times."

"I'm sorry."

"Don't be. I've worked with dozens of writers over the years. Many of them are insecure about their work. You'd be surprised how many of my best-selling authors still struggle with this. Guess it goes with being an artist."

Diane could hardly believe Frieda used that word. Was she really an *artist*?

"Actually, what the editor was calling about, in a sense, was they liked it so much they want to see more."

"They want more books? That's good, right? Wait, you mean they want to see more completed books? But I've only finished the one I sent in. I've been working on some more ideas but—"

"Well, that's what the editor said, but there's more to it. There's a good-news, bad-news side to this development. The good news is that they really do like your book. Not just the editor we've been working with, but the whole publishing committee."

Diane braced herself for the bad news.

"But there were some strong voices on the committee expressing concern that you only have the one book written. With the economy as it is, everyone's being really careful these days about budget issues. It makes them not so willing to take risks on new authors."

"New, unknown authors," Diane added.

"Right. Some on the committee aren't so sure they should make the kind of investment this house usually makes with their authors unless they're certain you can turn out more books as good as this one."

"You mean, they're afraid I might be just a one-hit wonder?"

"Exactly. And they don't want that to happen. What they've come back with is a request for a three-book proposal."

"Three books?"

"That's the idea. The one you've written will be the first. But before they'll buy it, they want to see a proposal that includes two more. If they like what they see, they'll buy all three."

"And if they don't like the two new ones, the deal's off?"

There was a pause. "Maybe, maybe not," Frieda said. "But don't worry about that. Like me, the acquisitions editor's been at this a long time. We know a good writer when we see one. We know you can do this. She even said that if they liked only one of the two newer books, she'd work with us to help come up with a third the committee would buy. That's really a good thing, Diane. She's totally on our side here."

Diane was feeling excited by this and a little terrified. "So, do I have to write two complete books? How much—"

"No, no—just proposals. But they'll have to be pretty complete, with all the main characters and plot points thought through, and a solid ending. For both stories. Maybe ten pages of material for each new book."

That wouldn't be too hard, Diane thought. She'd written something like that for the first book. "What kind of time frame are we talking about?"

"That's just it. We'd need you to get right on this. The editor wants to come back to the committee within a month. Do you think that's possible?"

A month, Diane thought. It seemed like something she could do. But how could she know? She'd never done anything like this before. Writing novels was so different than newspaper reporting.

"There's another upside to all this, Diane. If they like what we send, as I said, they'll make this a three-book contract, which means three times the money in the advance, and a much stronger time commitment from the publisher."

"Wow."

Diane so wished Eric was here to discuss this. But as soon as she thought that, she instantly knew what he would say. She could almost see his face, all lit up, saying, *Do it, Diane. It's something you've wanted to do for as long as I've known you. You'll never know until you try. But I know you can do it.*

"What do you think, Diane? Are you up for this?"

"I'll do it," she said. "Tell the editor I'll get to work on it as soon as we get off the phone."

"Great. I know you can do this. You've laid a great foundation with this first book. Really strong characters. If you'd like to run any ideas by me as you go, just give me a call."

"Do you know what they're looking for? Do they want me to do a series or three separate mystery stories?"

"Let's think about a series, a trilogy maybe. The same main characters working on some brand-new cases, or at least keep things in the same location. I love the setting for this first story. But...let's not go into the details here. You give it some time, let the creative juices flow. I'm sure some wonderful ideas will present themselves."

"I hope you're right."

"I know I am. And I'll be here, so just call me whenever you need to."

Diane hit End and sat back in her chair.

She looked down at Rocky. He seemed to notice and looked up at her briefly. "They want a three-book proposal, Rocky." He cocked his head to the side. "You know what this means?" His mouth opened, his tongue hung off to one side. He made that face he always made, the one that seemed so close to a smile. "No, I don't suppose you do." He got up and hurried to her side. She patted his head as he leaned against her.

Thank You, God, for Rocky. Rocky didn't have the right words to say, but he knew when she needed a hug. He gave up chewing on that rawhide for her without hesitation and, judging by its looks, he'd had it right where he'd wanted it. She leaned down and kissed the top of his head. His tail thumped against the floor.

So much for chopping onions and peppers and that delicious recipe she had planned to try out tonight. She'd either have to order takeout or head down to Main Street in a few hours and grab a bite to eat. It was time to get to work.

A three-book proposal. She knew she should be excited. There really were, as Frieda called them, some serious upsides to this. The publisher wasn't rejecting her—they wanted to see *more* of her work. They were willing to spend money on her and to invest in her career as a novelist. That was a good thing, a great thing even. They just wanted to make sure she could sustain the quality level in future books they had seen in this first one. Nothing wrong with that.

But what if she couldn't pull it off? What if she *was* just a one-hit wonder? What if this book was the climax of years of writing desire and creativity, and she'd used it all up on this one effort...and now the well had run dry?

She had a number of other ideas sketched out, other mystery stories, other heroes and heroines, possible plot twists and such. Some she really liked. But until a few moments ago, she thought she had all the time in the world to let them simmer, then pull them together at a casual pace while she did things like sit in a comfy chair, drink coffee, and listen to soothing music.

Her whole career as a journalist had been about writing under pressure, with deadlines always hovering over her head. She let out a tense sigh and stood, then walked back to her bedroom to get her notebooks. Rocky padded right behind her.

"This is a good thing, Rocky."

Chapter Six

Nap time was a gift from God.

Shelley knew that having thoughts that actually made it all the way through her head in one piece was a rare treat. Rarer still were those moments when both children were asleep at the same time. Added to the mix, perhaps the most shocking thing, was that Prize was lying quietly outside in the backyard.

For the last twenty minutes, she'd been sitting at her beloved mission oak table, bequeathed to her by her grandmother, writing out all the ideas that had sprung from her talk earlier today with Madeleine Bancroft. Marble Cove's fall fair was the perfect launching pad for her new baking business. As the list of ideas grew, she became more excited about the possibilities. Not for the fair, really, but for her baking business. But the list also fueled a growing feeling of being overwhelmed. Each idea seemed to generate its own list of to-dos.

Shelley tried to block those anxious thoughts before they got a firm hold, reminding herself that she was not alone. God would help her, and so would her friends ... especially Diane. She'd said as much over the Labor Day weekend.

Now that her book was safely in the publisher's hands, Diane said she'd have a nice lull in her schedule as she waited for them to send it back to edit. Shelley was sure Diane would come up with things Shelley had forgotten to add and find plenty of shortcuts for things she'd already written down.

An added benefit to all this, she hoped, would be an end to the not-so-subtle jabs from her mother-in-law, implying Shelley wasn't doing all she could to ease their financial stress. She had started in again at the family's Labor Day cookout.

She heard a noise outside, a familiar one. It sounded like Dan's pickup pulling into the driveway. This couldn't be good. She glanced at the clock on the microwave. He shouldn't be home for another hour. Quietly, she got up and looked out the living room window. It was Dan. As he opened the pickup truck door, she knew instantly from the look on his face what had happened.

Please don't let Prize start to bark, she prayed, as she hurried in her bare feet to the front door. She wanted to intercept Dan before he came in and woke up the kids. But as soon as the front door clicked, Prize heard it too, all the way from the backyard. She started barking and pawing at the kitchen door. A moment later, Shelley heard Emma starting to fuss in her crib.

She walked outside to greet Dan. The sidewalk chilled her feet.

When he saw her, he forced a smile. "Almost made it the whole day."

"Ran out of work?" she said, though she knew the answer.

He nodded. She hugged him. He left his arm around her shoulder as they walked back to the house. *This is nice,* she thought. She'd rather have Dan working steadily, but this was pleasant too. They stepped up to the door. Emma's fussing graduated to crying and now almost matched the volume of Prize's barking.

"What are you doing out here in your bare feet?" he asked.

"Well, up until a moment ago, the kids were both down for a nap, and I didn't want to make a sound." She closed the front door behind them.

"I'm sorry," he said. Now Aiden was beginning to stir. "I'm causing all kinds of trouble." He set his lunch box on the coffee table.

"It's not your fault," she said. He couldn't help being let off early. He looked so discouraged. "They were bound to wake up for something."

He walked out to the dining area, saw the cup of coffee, and picked up the list she was making at the table.

"The coffee's still fresh," she said. "Do you want me to fix you a cup?"

"Better not. I've been drinking it all afternoon."

She knew what that meant. Work had been slow for hours.

"What are you working on here, a shopping list?"

She rushed over to show him. "No, it's a list of things I need to do to launch my baking business."

"How's it coming?"

Emma let out an even louder cry. "I better get her."

"No, you keep working on that. I'll get her." He started toward the hall.

"She'll need her diaper changed."

"Oh." He stopped, then turned around and grinned.

"How about I go change her, and then you watch her for a little while?" Shelley smiled back.

"I can do that."

A few minutes later, she came back down the hall and put Emma in his arms.

"You're being followed," Dan said.

She turned around.

"I got up too, Mommy," Aiden said. "Daddy, you came home."

"Yes, I did."

"Can I watch Veggie Tales?"

"You want some apple juice first?" Shelley asked.

He nodded.

"Let me get that," Dan said.

"Really?"

"Sure." He carried Emma into the living room, with Aiden following behind. "I'm tired of sitting around with nothing useful to do."

"Okay..." She looked down at her list, then had an idea. "Dan, would you mind terribly if I went over to Diane's for about twenty minutes to run some of this by her?"

"We're good here."

She got up and dropped her list into her purse. "I won't be long." She gave him a peck on the cheek and hurried out before the kids made a fuss.

The air was crisp and cool as she made her way across the street. The sun had started its descent, but it was still nice and bright. For some reason, she wasn't that depressed about Dan coming home early. Normally, it would have been enough to send her spiraling downward. Maybe it was the changes she was starting to see in him. Maybe it was the list in her purse—putting it together had actually made the baking business seem more real.

Or maybe she was beginning to learn to trust God a little more than she used to.

★   ★   ★

Diane was so deep in thought, reading through one of her book ideas, that she barely heard the doorbell ring. She did clearly hear Rocky barking. He ran down the hall to get her. She looked up and saw him standing in the doorway. "What is it, boy? Someone at the door?" He ran back toward the living room.

She went to the window and peeked out, but she couldn't see who it was. She was hurrying down the hall when the doorbell rang again. "Just a minute," she yelled to whoever it was. "Okay, Rocky, you sit right there. Sit...sit..." She was trying to reel in his over-the-top hospitality. "Good boy."

As the door opened, there stood Shelley, a big smile on her face. "Hey, Diane. Hope I'm not interrupting anything."

"No, come on in." Diane looked around her. "The kids aren't with you?"

"Dan's watching them across the street." Shelley stepped inside.

"I'm sorry," Diane said, shutting the door. "I guess that means there's no work again?"

"Well, he almost made it until the end of the day." She set her purse down on the coffee table and pulled out a piece of paper. "But I'm so excited. I've brought this over to show you."

"What is it? Can I get you something to drink? Some coffee?"

"No, thanks, I just finished a cup. I really can't stay too long. I have to get dinner started soon. But I had to run this by you." She held the paper up. "Maybe I could leave it with you, and you could look it over tonight. I know I won't have any more time left today to fiddle with it."

"Well, have a seat, and let me see it. What is it?"

"It's a list I put together this afternoon, a bunch of ideas to help get my baking business started. I'm so excited!" She handed it to Diane and sat on the sofa. "I know you mentioned over the weekend you wanted to help me get things going on this. Then this morning I was talking with Madeleine Bancroft. Don't think you know her. She's . . . well, that's a long story. Anyway, she reminded me about the fall fair coming up. Have you been to it before? It's just three weeks away."

"Eric and I did get to the fair a couple of times. But it's been a few years." Already Diane was starting to feel edgy. What with this urgent need to get the proposals whipped together, she'd forgotten all about what she'd promised Shelley. She glanced down at the list.

"It suddenly dawned on me...the fair would be the perfect place to launch my baking business. Hundreds of people will be there, maybe thousands. All kinds of tourists, and almost everyone in town shows up. All the restaurants get involved, and they have that annual bake-off contest. Did you ever stick around for that?"

"Once," Diane said.

"I was thinking, what if I baked one of my best cakes or pies? Maybe I could make it to the final round. Wouldn't that be a great way to get attention for the business?"

"I think you'd do better than that, Shelley. You could win the whole thing."

Shelley made a "hope-so" face. "Maddie reminded me that they let all kinds of vendors come in and set up tables on the side streets. I could bake a whole bunch of things and sell them there. Or maybe just give away free samples at the table while we hand out brochures about my new business. And on the brochures, we could tell all about my Web site. Have pictures made of everything. I've been looking into it. It's kind of hard to imagine, but there's all kind of Web sites now with people selling desserts—cupcakes, pies...all kinds of things—and they ship them in the mail, if you can believe that."

"Oh, I can believe it. I've ordered baked goods for friends over the Internet before. And someone sent me the most amazing cheese Danishes last year."

"See?" Shelley said. "I've got a wonderful recipe for cheese Danishes."

Diane was dying inside. Shelley was so excited. How could she let her friend down like this? She'd said yes to Frieda about dropping everything to work on this new book proposal. Now she'd have no time to help Shelley. "You mentioned having brochures and a Web site. You haven't done anything with these yet, have—"

"No, but I've got them down there on my list. See them? Right near the top. I don't know a thing about graphic design or Web sites. But I was thinking maybe you could look this over, and we could divide up the list between things I could do and things you're better at. I know Margaret and Beverly said they'd like to help some. Maybe we could think of some things they could do too."

Diane sighed. This was so hard.

"I was also thinking," Shelley continued, "as you looked it over, you might turn up some things I missed, or maybe you'd have some shortcuts to save time. The fair's only three weeks away, but I thought if we got it all organized..." She stopped and looked at Diane. "What's wrong, Diane? Is everything okay? Just listen to me, going on and on here."

"It's not you, Shelley."

"But you seem... Is this a bad time? I know this is a lot, and I don't mean to be—"

"Really, Shelley, you don't need to apologize. Something has come up, something pretty big. It just happened a little while ago."

"I'm sorry. Can I help? Do you want to talk about it?"

Diane sighed again. How could she say this? Shelley was so happy and excited. She looked into her eyes. "I got a phone call from my agent. There's been a setback of sorts."

"With your book? Oh, Diane, I'm so sorry."

"No, it's not bad news. In fact, it's good news, really. They still want to publish my book. And actually, they want me to write three books for them."

"Really? Diane, that's wonderful!"

"It is, mostly. But...I'm very nervous about getting this right. I know I said I'd help you, but..."

There was a long pause. The expression on Shelley's face revealed she was beginning to understand.

"But I can still do some of this," Diane said quickly. "I'm hoping these proposals will come very quickly. If I can—"

"Proposals?"

Diane explained the whole situation with the three-book proposal. As she did, Shelley's countenance grew steadily more concerned.

"That's it, then," Shelley said. "I guess I missed God completely. I thought He'd given me this brilliant idea, but there's no way I can do half the things on that list. I'm no Maddie Bancroft."

"I'm so sorry, Shelley. I hate, absolutely hate, telling you this." Diane felt like she was about to cry. "It's just, the timing is bad. Like I said, I'll get these things whipped together, and then I'll take half that list as soon as—"

"No, it's okay. You haven't done anything wrong. I know you'd help me if you could." Shelley picked up the list Diane had laid on the coffee table. "And really, I'm happy for you. A three-book deal. That's even better than what you had before. I don't want you to rush them just to help me." She paused. "I just need to rethink this whole thing. Maybe I'm not supposed to do this baking business, after all."

"Don't say that, Shelley. You're a wonderful baker, and I think it really could work."

"But I don't know a thing about business," she said. "And neither does Dan."

Diane thought a moment. "I've got an idea, maybe a way this could still work."

"What is it?"

"If I can't do it, that doesn't mean someone else can't. How about I go down tomorrow to the *Courier,* put a classified ad in the paper? Maybe there's someone in Marble Cove we don't know who we can hire to do the Web site and brochures."

"But I don't have any money, Diane."

"No, but I do. And I—"

"Dan would never be okay with you paying for something like that. I'm not sure I'd be okay with it, either."

"I wouldn't be paying for something. I'd be making an investment. It's called venture capital. People do this all the time in business. I'd put the money up for this, and you can pay me back down the road after your business takes off. I could even write up something to make it sound professional and legal. Or maybe Beverly can."

"I don't know, Diane. It's sweet of you to offer. But—"

"Just let me try. An ad costs hardly anything. You don't have to tell Dan about it just yet. We'll run the ad in the *Courier*, see if anyone responds. We'll find out how much it costs to hire someone, and then you two talk about it and decide."

The slightest glimmer of hope appeared in Shelley's eyes. "I guess that can't hurt."

"Meanwhile," Diane said, "I saw something on that checklist you could start looking into."

"Which one?" Shelley began looking over the list.

"It's down there near the bottom," Diane said. "Every city has its own laws about doing a business out of your home. See what you can find out about what's involved, what kind of permits you might need. If all this comes together, you're going to be doing a lot of baking across the street in the next three weeks."

CHAPTER SEVEN

Diane didn't sleep well at all that night. Half the time was spent wrestling with book ideas for the new proposal, the other half fighting off guilt feelings for letting Shelley down. The dawn's morning light seemed to take forever to arrive.

For the last few hours of the morning, she had tried unsuccessfully to make progress on her proposals. It probably didn't help that she'd skipped breakfast. If she couldn't replenish her energy from sleep, she at least needed to eat some food. And she certainly didn't want to throw her blood sugar off. Hypoglycemia was nothing to mess with. She had stood in front of the pantry for several minutes, then just as long in front of the fridge. Nothing she saw in either location would do.

Then something she and Shelley had talked about the day before came back to her. She wanted something that could be found only in the pastry cabinet down at the Cove. She saw it in her mind like a photograph. A delicious cheese Danish with a zigzagging dribble of white icing. It was almost calling her name.

"That's it, Rocky. There's no point in sitting here another minute." Eric would tell her to go for it. She sighed as she packed her notebooks in her brief bag. She missed him so much, and the fun things he'd say at any given moment, things so unlike her.

She knew a good part of her tendency to fret over things lately, even her nighttime battles with insomnia, had their roots in spending too much time alone.

Rocky followed her down the hall and out into the living room. "I love you, Rocky, but you're just not much of a conversationalist."

She had read something in a women's magazine article last week that really rang true with her. Its target audience was women who lived alone—either through divorce or as widows—after living many years with a husband. One of the issues the article raised was that women, on average, say twenty-thousand words a day. At first, it had sounded like an absurd number to Diane, so she'd looked it up on the Internet. That seemed to be the generally accepted number. Did she really talk that much...ever?

The article went on to say that, even if your man wasn't a great conversationalist, as a minimum, his presence in your life was good for your mental health, allowing you to keep the words flowing out of your mouth so they didn't get stuck in your head. One of the unfortunate consequences of living alone was not having someone with whom to air out all the thoughts and ideas swirling inside.

Of course, the goal of the article was an appeal for women to get outside, join a club, do crafts, make some good friends, male or female. In other words, stay connected to people— in person, on the phone, and over the Internet. Which was another reason Diane so cherished her friends, the Marble Cove Miracle Club, as she'd started to think of the little group. It was why she couldn't let herself be pulled away from them. Not even by a good thing like this new book deal.

Her friends had all said, in different ways and at different times, how much she had helped them and how much they cherished her friendship. But she needed them every bit as much. She thought again of that look on Shelley's face when Diane had said she couldn't help as much right away. She couldn't let these new deadlines drive her into a life of isolation and loneliness.

She let Rocky out for a few minutes and freshened his water bowl. When he came back in, she patted him on the head, grabbed her purse and brief bag, put on a sweater, and headed out the door.

Destination? The Cove. And they had better have at least one cheese Danish left in that pastry cabinet.

★　　★　　★

The lighthouse painting was coming along nicely. As best she could tell, Margaret was even a little ahead of schedule. It helped that customer traffic at the gallery had been light that morning. She swiveled in her stool away from the painting toward the gallery and the front door. No one was even in the store right now.

It was funny in a way. Seeing an empty gallery back in July would have made her nervous, maybe downright depressed.

She thanked God that Matt Beauregard and his daughter had come to the store that day. It meant that not having customers in the store was actually a good thing: more time to work on her lighthouse paintings for Lighting the Way, and more inventory on hand for Marble Cove's fall fair less than three weeks away. Her eyes focused on the flyer taped to the front window.

She got up and walked into the gallery. Time to stretch her legs and freshen her coffee. The words of Councilman Bert Atwood replayed in her head: *"Of course, looking around your place here, you might get* all *your paintings out there on the sidewalk."*

Three weeks away.

There didn't seem to be enough time to keep her deadlines with the lighthouse paintings on track and replenish the gallery with works she could sell to individual customers. She could redo paintings she'd already done before. That would save a little bit of time, but it wasn't nearly enough. She might just have to call all those other artists and get some more consignment work in here.

A tapping sound interrupted her thoughts. She turned to find Diane standing by the storefront window. "I'm on my way to the Cove," Diane called through the glass. "I saw you standing there and had to say hi."

Margaret motioned for her to come in. Diane hesitated. "Just for a minute," Margaret yelled. "I want to run something by you."

"Okay." Diane came inside, and they hugged. "This had better not cost me my cheese Danish," she said, smiling.

"Cheese Danish?"

"Shelley and I talked about cheese Danishes yesterday, and it stuck with me. I was just on my way to the Cove to get one. I'm getting anxious someone might snatch the last one. Plus, I gotta keep my blood sugar up, you know?"

Margaret laughed. "This won't take long." She walked her to the center of the gallery. "Spin around the room slowly, and tell me what you see."

"Okay." Diane obeyed. "I see...a number of incredible paintings by a talented artist and friend. And some other nice paintings and sculptures by some other artists I don't know. I see some great furniture by a local craftsman who might just be related to that aforementioned artist and friend."

"I mean, something...negative. Tell me something that looks like a problem to you."

"Do I have to spin around again?"

Margaret laughed. "No."

"Wait—there are no customers in the gallery?"

"I'm actually glad for that right now," Margaret said. "No. Something else."

"Okay, let's see." Diane seemed to be studying the situation. An expression came over her face, as if the lights had just turned on. "I see a lot of blank spaces where paintings use to be."

"That's the one," Margaret said. She explained her dilemma to Diane, including Bert Atwood's observations. The expression on Diane's face did not coincide with the problems Margaret shared. Her face registered no concern at all. If anything, the more Margaret talked, the brighter Diane's face became. "Why are you smiling?" Margaret said.

"I'm thinking of a fairly simple solution that will make every problem you just described disappear."

"See, I knew I just needed to talk this over with you. What is it?"

"*Giclée* prints."

"Zhee-*what*?"

"It's a French word, I think," Diane said. "It's spelled with a G but pronounced zhee-clay."

"What are they, and how can they help me with this problem?"

"Eric and I spent one of our anniversaries in Charleston, South Carolina. I don't know why I haven't thought of it before. They have all kinds of art galleries down there. You'd love it. We'd see some paintings that cost several thousand dollars and others just a few hundred. Even some smaller ones for less than a hundred dollars."

"For original paintings?" Margaret asked.

"No, the most expensive ones were, but most of them were giclée prints. Look it up on the Internet: I'm sure you'll find all kinds of things about it. They look like paintings, but they're prints—done right on canvas. I think they use some kind of special ink jet printer, or something."

"And people will pay hundreds of dollars for them? For just a printout?"

Diane nodded. "You've got to think about it this way. Didn't you tell me how much it bothered you that so many customers come in, love one of your paintings, but leave because they can't afford it?"

"Yes. It happens way too much. When I ask them how much they can afford, I'd go broke if I sold it for that little."

"Well, see, this would solve that too. You could sell these prints for a price they could afford. They'd walk out with a painting they'd love, and you'd make a decent profit off every one."

"People wouldn't mind that they're just getting a copy?"

"Some people might, but most wouldn't care about that. Here's another thing you could do with these. We saw this a lot down in Charleston. An artist would print only a limited number of copies, say twenty-five or fifty, maybe two hundred of a smaller one. I'm just guessing here. And they'd sign each print separately, and on back write, 'Print number five of fifty' or something. You could even design an official-looking certificate of authenticity. One artist also touched up each painting by hand, just a few obvious brush strokes here and there, to give each print something of a unique stamp. And it's right on canvas, so it feels like a real painting to the buyer."

Margaret's smile began to match Diane's. "I can see something like that really working."

"Of course it can work. We almost bought a painting—well, a giclée print—for three hundred dollars."

"You did?"

"Almost."

"Why almost?"

"Eric bought me an antique emerald ring instead. I'll have to show it to you sometime. But people pay that all the time for fine works of art. And that's what you have here, Margaret."

Margaret looked around at her paintings, tried to imagine them being worth all that money to someone else...as a print.

"And another thing," Diane said. "Once you set this up, you should start charging a lot more money for your originals. Like double, at least. You wouldn't sell them as often, but you wouldn't need to because of what you'd be making on the prints."

"Oh, Diane, this is a wonderful idea. Thank you so much for stopping in." Margaret gave her a big hug. "I really think this idea could work."

"I know it can," Diane said. "I just wish I could help everyone so quickly."

Margaret was about to ask what that meant, when a thought hit her like a screen door slapping shut in the wind. "Oh no."

"What's the matter?" Diane asked.

"It's a great idea, but when will I ever have the time to pull it off? I'm bogged down as it is. And the fall fair is only three weeks away."

"Couldn't Allan help you?"

"I don't want to ask him. He's added several new customers since we started putting samples of his work here in the gallery."

"Oh."

"Is there any chance you could help? I remember you said that now that you sent your book off to the publisher, you're in kind of a lull. I heard you tell Shelley you were going to help her get her baking business organized." Diane's expression changed, as if Margaret had just shared some bad news. "What's wrong? I'm not thinking we'd have to get this whole idea put together by the fall fair. But maybe we could—"

"I don't think I'll be able to help you," Diane said.

"You can't...at all?"

"Oh, Margaret. Maybe a little, but..."

"What is it?"

"Yesterday, I had to disappoint Shelley, and now I'm letting you down."

"What's wrong, Diane? What's happened?"

"It's nothing bad, really. In fact, it's good, I think. It just has me flustered. I can't think of anything else. I can't even sleep." Diane went on to explain all about the sudden change in her book deal, and all the work that went along with it. "They want this whole proposal done in less than a month," she said, "and I don't even know where to begin."

"Oh, you poor dear," Margaret said. "Listen, don't you worry about me. You've done your job. You've given me a wonderfully exciting idea to start praying about. I'll talk it over with Allan. Maybe he can come up with a way to get things started. Or maybe we'll just have to wait awhile, do this giclée print project down the road a ways."

"I'm so sorry," Diane said. "I keep thinking I can get these proposals done quickly and then be right back to helping everyone."

"There's no reason for you to feel guilty. This is a wonderful thing, Diane. Take your time on this and do a good job. Just think about it: God has given us both the opportunity to fulfill our dreams. You at your age and me...a whole lot older."

Diane laughed. "It is a wonderful thing. I'm just not so sure I like the idea of writing under deadlines again."

"I know what you mean there," Margaret said. She chuckled. "I was thinking the very same thing, but about my painting." She smiled as a thought came to mind. "You know what our problem is, Diane? You and me? We're victims of our own success! That's all there is to it." They both laughed. "So you're headed next door to the Cove?"

"Yes, and I better get a move on it."

"Before someone grabs the last cheese Danish," Margaret said.

CHAPTER EIGHT

Diane had barely gotten out of the Shearwater Gallery when she remembered something else she was supposed to do downtown today. A young mother pushing a stroller across the street put it back in her mind. *Shelley.* She was supposed to stop off at the *Marble Cove Courier* and put that ad in the paper for Shelley in hopes of finding someone in Marble Cove they could hire to make brochures and a Web site for her baking business.

That gave Diane another idea. She ducked back into the gallery a minute. As she opened the glass door, she saw Margaret walking back to her studio. "Margaret, there's something I forgot to ask you a moment ago." Margaret turned. "I'm heading over to the *Courier* just now to place an ad in the paper for Shelley. Do you want me to put one in for you too?"

"An ad? Whatever for?"

"A help-wanted ad. Since I can't help Shelley set up her baking business like I promised, I told her I'd run an ad in the *Courier* to see if someone else in Marble Cove knew how to do things like that. I could do the same for you to see if we can get someone to help you get started doing the art prints in here."

Margaret smiled. "It's nice of you to offer, Diane, but I think I need some more time to think this one over. I'm not even sure if I have the money to hire someone just yet. I really do like the idea though."

"No problem," Diane said. "I don't mean to pressure you about it."

"What happened to your getting to work on that new proposal?"

"I'm still planning on it, but I remembered I needed to do this first. And I feel like I owe everyone a little bit of effort because I can't help out right now like I told you all I could. Besides, they don't run the *Courier* but once a week now, on Saturdays. I checked, and today's the last day to get ads in for the next issue."

They exchanged good-byes, and Diane walked to the Cove, ate the last delicious Danish, and continued around the block until she stood in front of the offices for the *Marble Cove Courier.* A few copies of the latest issue sat in a red metal rack off to the right. It was a free publication, sustained by classified ads and, of course, the ads from almost every local vendor in town. A few of the bigger groceries outside of town regularly inserted flyers with weekly specials. The *Courier* didn't bother with national news or even state news unless it directly affected the residents of Marble Cove.

Diane had always loved to read it. She'd even had it mailed to her house in Cambridge every week before she'd moved here. It helped her stay in touch with the latest small-town news. And of course, people loved to see their names appear in the paper—or better still, to have their picture show up in the pages. Most of the downtown businesses had articles cut out and pinned to little bulletin boards not far from their cash registers. These articles celebrated their special moments, such as when they'd won some kind of award, had some big store anniversary, or served their thousandth customer.

Diane glanced down at the latest issue. The headline read: *Fall Fair Just Around the Corner!* Beneath the headline, Samantha Bailey, last year's bake-off contest winner, beamed at the camera. Diane smiled as she reached for the door handle. That was timely, since she was there about Shelley's baking business.

She stepped up and inside the front office, then walked to the counter. Three glass panels framed in oak allowed her to see into the next room. Over on the left, his eyes fixed to a large flat-screen monitor, sat Gerald Kimball, Marble Cove's lone reporter. Gerald was tall, in his midforties, and a little wide in the waist, but he didn't appear overweight anywhere else. He was mostly bald on top except for a little tuft of hair in front that refused to surrender its hold.

A bell over the door rang when Diane walked in, but Gerald didn't seem to hear it. Gerald sat where Abby Lane, the paper's office manager, usually did, but Diane didn't see Abby anywhere in sight.

Diane had met Gerald a few years back. In that first chat, he'd learned that she'd worked as a reporter in Cambridge. He seemed taken aback by this, perhaps a little intimidated. Diane had wondered if he might have struggled, comparing the kind of "big league" stories she reported on versus his small-town neighbor assignments. She'd gone out of her way to assure him then, and the few other times they'd talked, how much she loved reading his stories in the *Courier*.

She made a little noise with her feet, but he still didn't hear. That's when she noticed a little brass bell on the left side of the counter and a note behind it: "Ring for Service." Banging it once was enough—it was so loud it startled her.

"Just a minute," she heard Gerald yell from the next room, his face still glued to the screen. It looked like some kind of desktop publishing program. "Be right they-ah." She knew what it was like to be so close to finishing an article that you hated to be interrupted.

"Oh, Mrs. Spencer, it's you," he said, as he walked toward the counter.

"Hi, Gerald. Don't you remember, the last time we talked you said you'd start calling me Diane?" She enjoyed the way his Maine accent rendered her last name, but he couldn't be more than ten years younger; he made her feel so old calling her "Mrs. *Spenc-ah*."

"That's right...Diane. I did. So what can I do for you?"

"I'd like to put a help-wanted ad in the *Courier*. But before I do that, I wondered if you might know someone who could do what I need. You've lived in Marble Cove a long time."

"All my life. What do you need help with?"

"Do you know Shelley Bauer, a young mother who lives on my street?"

"Shelley and Dan Bauer. Don't know them well, but, yes, I know them."

"Shelley's looking to start a baking business."

"Is it somewhere in town here?"

"Well, not exactly. More of an online business. Maybe some local stuff too."

"It's amazing what you can get online these days."

"Isn't it?" she said. "She was hoping to get most of it launched in time for the fall fair."

"I'm working on an article about that very thing just now," he said. "Writing a few stories, as a matter of fact."

"So I'm wondering if there's someone in town who's good on the Internet, knows how to make brochures, and can maybe help her set up a Web site. Do you know anyone like that?"

"*Hmm.*"

"I imagine you're pretty good at that sort of thing," she said.

"I am...a little. I do most of my work on the computer too. Usually from home though. Of course, Abby does most of the day-to-day operations around here. I think you've met her. She's gone for the week. She combined a few vacation days with the holiday. I'm filling in. I figured I could work here just as well as home. So you see...I'm wicked-busy these days, trying to get the paper out on time. We drop down to a weekly after Labor Day, but with the fall fair just three weeks away, I don't think I could do any freelance work right now."

"I'm sure you are. It was foolish of me to ask." She was sure her implication that he had nothing but time on his hands hadn't made him feel less intimidated by her.

"No, it never hurts to ask."

"Well, do you know anyone else in town who might help? I'd be willing to pay. I'm not looking for volunteers."

"No one comes to mind right off the top of my head."

"Then I guess I better go with the ad. How do I go about that?"

"Right over there." He pointed over her shoulder. "See that little desk? We set it up this week just for folks wanting to put ads in the classified. That's mostly why people come in here to the office."

She turned and saw a desk in the corner by the front window. "That's what I'll do then. Thanks."

"Do you see that box of forms? I wrote a little paragraph and taped it just above it there to explain what's what. You can make the ads as big or small as you like, or pay a little more to add special features. You can put things in bold or italics or maybe a bigger font. I'm sure it will be nothing for someone like you to figure out."

"Thanks, Gerald. That's what I'll do." She walked over to the desk, then remembered something and walked back to the counter. "Gerald, you said you were pretty busy working on stories about the fall fair. But I also know the *Courier* likes to feature big things that have happened to local residents."

"Folks love that sort of thing," he said.

"Have you heard about what's happened with Margaret Hoskins?"

"No, is she all right? She's the artist, right? Opened that gallery around the corner a few months ago?"

"That's her. No, she's fine."

"I just saw her this morning," he said. "Seemed fine to me."

"She is. I'm referring to a big contract she got recently from a major greeting card company called Lighting the Way."

"You don't say."

"Yes. The CEO of the company visited Marble Cove a while back and walked into Margaret's gallery. He liked several of her paintings—came back and bought a boatload of them to use in a brand-new series of cards featuring different lighthouses. Then he contacted her later to commission several new paintings."

"Really? I'd love to do a story on something like that. The next break I get, I'll head over there and talk to her. And I'll bring my camera too. Something like that might make the front page. Does she have any of those lighthouse paintings finished yet?"

"I think she's finishing up the first new one right now."

"Speaking of lighthouses...Abby was telling me we had a young man come in here the last several weeks, asking all kinds of questions about Orlean Point Light. About its history and such. He was wondering if we had any old newspaper articles about it."

"Really?"

"I heard you and some of your friends have been quite interested in the lighthouse. Abby said you spent a good while upstairs in the morgue."

"We did, back in July. Looking for articles from the thirties. Do you know who this man is or where he's from?"

"No. I didn't actually meet him myself. Abby thought he was from away. Never saw him before. If she said his name, I don't recall it. Guess he spent a good while upstairs too. When he came down, she sent him over to the library, thought he might find more information there. I asked her if he was a reporter. She said no. I thought he might be doing research for a book, the way he was writing everything down, and the kind of questions he was asking."

"Did she say what kind of questions? Can you remember if he asked anything specific?"

Gerald pondered a moment. "She said he did ask about one fellow in particular. She only remembered it because the name was rather odd."

"Do you remember what it was?"

"What was it now...? She told me, and I thought it was an odd name too. Edward something. Oh, shoot, what was it?"

"Was it Edward Maker?"

"That's it!" he said, eyes wide. "Edward Maker. An odd name for these parts, don't you think?"

This was so exciting. Diane wondered who could this man be. Could he possibly be the mystery man going in and out of the lighthouse? He had to be. But she wondered what his connection was to Edward Maker. How did he know about him? How much did he know?

"By the way," Gerald said, "I talked to Detective Little last week. He tells me you've got some big news yourself. Some kind of a major book deal with a publisher down in New York City."

"Well, the contract with the publisher isn't signed yet, but a pretty big publisher told my agent they like my first book and want to publish it."

"You sound a little iffy there," he said. "I know a little about publishing. From what I've read, things move pretty slow."

"Actually, I wish things would slow down a little bit." Diane gave him a brief overview of her dilemma with the three-book proposal.

"If you ask me," he said when she finished, "that seems like a good problem to have."

"I know, Gerald. I keep telling myself that."

"It sounds like something for the *Courier,* if you're interested. It wouldn't exactly be a local-makes-good story, since you've only been living here a few months. But still, folks around here might think it was something pretty special. It's like Marble Cove had its own Stephen King living right here."

Diane chuckled at the comparison. "I certainly wouldn't mind having his sales. Let's just say that my story has a great deal less gore. I can confidently say it's not the same readership."

"A story in the *Courier* might get a few folks to go out and buy it."

"That's very kind of you, Gerald. But I don't think I'd want that kind of attention right now. Maybe later, when the first book is ready to come out."

"Well, you just let me know, you hear?"

"I will." She sat down at the desk, and he turned to head back to his computer. "Oh, and Gerald, just a quick question about that man who was in here asking about the lighthouse."

"What's that?"

"Do you remember when he was in here last?"

He thought a moment. "You'd have to ask Abby, but it sounded like it was sometime last week. Now that I know you're interested, I'll pay more attention if he comes in again while I'm here."

"Thanks." She pulled a form for the classified ad out of the box and set it on the desk, but she had the hardest time focusing on what she should say. All she could think about was this mysterious young man and how she wished she had the time to dig into this exciting new development.

There had to be a connection though. Why else would he ask about Edward Maker? Diane instantly remembered the initials "EM" they'd found etched into the lighthouse foundation, and the partial date from the 1930s. And of course the phrase, "I'm sorry."

Her friends just had to hear about this.

CHAPTER NINE

Diane got Shelley's ad put together just the way she wanted. She dropped it into the box and headed out the door, intending to go back around the corner to the Cove to work on her proposal.

When she reached the corner, she noticed an older man waving at someone across the street. The sun was glaring, so she shielded her eyes to look more closely. It was August Jackson, and he was waving at her. What could he possibly want?

She looked down the street at the sign for the Cove, then back at August Jackson. She returned the wave. August was a retired reporter. He'd actually held the same job as Gerald Kimball many years ago.

August Jackson waved again. "Mrs. Spencer, a word with you, if you have a moment."

"Hello, Mr. Jackson," she said. "I'll be right there." He'd insisted she call him Augie, just as she had insisted he call her Diane, so she would have to remind him again. She waited for a UPS truck to pass, and she crossed the street. She stepped over the curb and stood next to him. This side of the street was completely shaded.

"Just come from the library," he said. "Seeing you there reminded me I had something to tell you. Something I think you'd find of interest." He backed up and sat on a bench against a brick wall between two shops. "Haven't seen you around much the last few weeks."

"I've been so busy finishing up my first novel, hardly even came outside to breathe." She sat beside him. "And now I've got another pressing project. Seems I can't do any of the things I'd like to do. But then, I can't really complain, seeing as I have a publisher interested in my book."

"Heard about that." Augie looked up over the black-framed glasses that sat low on his nose. He had on the same red plaid shirt and beaded leather moccasins he'd worn the last time she'd seen him. "What kind of novel are you writing, Mrs. Spencer?"

"Diane," she reminded him. "We're practically old friends now." Diane filled him in as briefly as she could. She told him about how the amateur sleuth in the first book determines to figure out what happened to the lighthouse keeper who vanished without a trace one hundred years ago. She also told him a little about her book proposal dilemma, hoping to drop a hint that she was in a hurry.

"Well, you must be thrilled. Did I ever tell you about the murder mystery I wrote once?"

"You did," Diane said.

"Could never sell it though. But look at you, selling not just one but three."

"Thanks, but they're not sold yet. And you're no slouch. Look at all the success you've had with your cookbooks."

Augie smiled. "'Course, who will ever know it's me, writing as Lucy Lamb?"

"You know, Augie, you should talk with your publisher. Times have changed. All kinds of men are into cooking these days. Some even have their own cooking shows." She smiled.

He smiled back, his thick white mustache spreading wider across his face. "You don't say. Well, I did talk to my publisher about going by my real name. We both agreed that I'm stuck. At my age, it's not a good time to start building a new readership. I'm afraid Lucy Lamb and I are forever united."

"So," Diane said in her businesslike voice, "what did you have to tell me? Was it something you read at the library?"

"Oh yes. The library. Wasn't something I read but someone I saw."

"Really? Who?"

"Some young fellow. Last week sometime. I don't recall what day. Actually, I saw him there once the week before that too."

Diane sat up straight. "Was it someone from Marble Cove?"

"No, he was from away. Apparently, he was doing research about the history of the lighthouse. He was asking all kinds of questions."

This had to be the same man, Diane thought. "Did you meet him? Did you catch his name?"

Augie nodded. "I did. Meet him, that is. He even told me his name. It went in one ear, right out the other. Happens all the time. So I just started calling him 'young man' after that. He didn't seem to mind. When you're pushing ninety, you can call a man in his forties 'young man' and get away with it. In fact, I did that very thing just—"

She glanced at her watch. "Augie, I'm in a little bit of a hurry. Can you tell me anything else about him? What did the two of you talk about?"

"Orlean Point Light, mostly. He told me he'd been over to the paper reading old articles about the lighthouse but couldn't find what he was looking for. I guess the years in question were the ones burned by that fire."

"The 1930s?"

"Why, yes, I believe it was."

"Did he happen to mention the name Edward Maker?"

August's eyes instantly reacted. "He did. Odd name, Maker. I told him it rang a bell, but not a very loud one. Long time ago. I told him all kinds of stories about the lighthouse, some of the better ones people tell over the years."

I'll bet you did, Diane thought.

"But he seemed kind of stuck on hearing about the 1930s mostly. I said I couldn't help too much with those years. I was a teen then and sick a good part of the time."

"Did you make the connection to the initials?" Diane asked.

"Initials?" He leaned forward on the bench.

"E.M. Remember, my friend Beverly and I talked to you about that? They're etched in the lighthouse foundation.

The same initials this young man talked about. You know, Edward Maker...E.M."

"Well, how about that?" He sat up and slapped his knee. "You're right. No, I didn't catch it at the time."

"Did you two talk about anything else?"

August thought a moment. "Nope. Think that was about it. He did spend several hours more in the library by himself. He was there when I left, if I recall."

Diane stood up. "Well, thanks, Augie. I'm glad you waved me over."

"I thought it might interest you."

"It most certainly does," she said. "If you see him again, will you let me know? Maybe try and get his name?"

"Will do."

They exchanged good-byes, and Diane headed back across the street. She knew she should go right to the Cove and work on that proposal, but this new information was too good to ignore.

She had to tell Beverly, Shelley, and Margaret.

$$\star \quad \star \quad \star$$

Diane stopped at the Shearwater Gallery, but apparently Margaret had locked up and gone home already. Diane headed in the same direction. Once back on Newport Avenue, she thought about stopping in at Shelley's, but a glance at her watch suggested that Shelley would be fixing dinner right now for a young, hungry family. Better not to disturb her.

As she angled toward Beverly's house, she saw Mrs. Peabody crossing the street. The elderly woman looked as if she was headed toward Beverly's too. Diane was a little surprised. She'd assumed that, now that Beverly had moved back to Marble Cove, she would no longer need Mrs. Peabody's help with her father. "Hello, Mrs. Peabody."

"Well, hello, Diane. Are you walking to the Wheelands'?"

"I am. Is that where you're headed?"

"Why, yes. To fix dinner. I thought I'd be all done with that now that Beverly's home. I guess she still needs me." She joined Diane on the sidewalk, and they walked side by side. She leaned closer and said conspiratorially, "Mr. Wheeland asked me not to mention it, but he prefers my cooking to Beverly's, I'm afraid."

"Did he say that?" Beverly had admitted she wasn't much of a cook, but Diane had a hard time believing her father would say this.

"Not in so many words," Mrs. Peabody admitted. "But in his own way, the mister made it quite clear. Women these days, so many working full-time outside the home. They don't have time to cultivate the culinary arts. I'm just happy to be able to help where I can."

"It probably has something to do with her needing time to unpack all those boxes," Diane said.

"I suppose."

They walked up to the door, and Diane knocked.

Beverly opened it. "Diane? I was expecting Mrs. Peabody— oh, hello, Mrs. Peabody! But Diane, what a nice surprise.

Come in." Beverly stood to one side, and Mrs. Peabody walked in.

"I can't stay," Diane said. "I just heard some—" She looked at Mrs. Peabody, instantly realizing how much she'd want to be in on any "news." Diane didn't really want to involve her in the conversation. She chose another word. "...some updates, on that project we've been working on. Can I speak to you about it out here?"

"Sure." Beverly turned to Mrs. Peabody. "You can go ahead and get started fixing dinner," she said. "But Father's taking a nap."

"I'll be quiet as a mouse," Mrs. Peabody said. She tiptoed down the hall.

"I'll be there in a minute." Beverly stepped outside and closed the door behind her. "So what's going on?"

Diane filled her in on her conversations with Gerald Kimball and August Jackson.

"A mysterious stranger," Beverly said when she'd finished. "How exciting."

"Isn't it?" Diane said.

"And our mystery man asked both men about Edward Maker?" Beverly said. "There has to be a connection to solving *our* little mystery at the lighthouse."

"I agree."

"I'll bet you this guy's the one who made those footprints in the sand by the lighthouse we found that night, just outside the hidden door."

"The ones that went in," Diane said, "but never came out."

"Exactly. It has to be. He's got to be the one who's been getting inside and causing those mysterious lights to appear. I wonder who he is."

"It looks like he's not keeping that a secret. He told Augie his name—but Augie forgot."

"I guess he didn't seem too mysterious to him," Beverly said. "But there's got to be a way for us to find out who he is and what he's up to. Oh, Diane, won't this be fun? A brand-new lead to follow. Uh...is something wrong?"

Diane didn't realize her expression had changed. "It would be exciting if I had the time to do it with you."

"I thought with your book turned in your schedule was supposed to lighten up."

"I thought so too. I have some new developments to share on that score too." Diane took a few minutes to fill Beverly in on her book news.

"Diane, I'm so happy for you!"

Her reaction made Diane freshly aware that this really was good news. Great news, even. "Thanks, Beverly. But I really wish there were a way I could do everything I'd been wanting to do with you three. I'd love to track down our mysterious stranger together."

"Well, don't worry about it. I've got some time, for a change. I'm off this week, and I've decided to keep Mrs. Peabody on to help me for the whole month at least. Let me think some more about this. We'll find a way to figure out who this mystery man is, see how he's connected to all that's been going on."

"And I'm hoping to be done with my proposals early to get back into the fun with you three. In the meantime, I know you'll think of something. But you have to promise to keep me in the loop."

Beverly smiled at her inquisitive friend. "I will."

CHAPTER TEN

O ver the next several days, things began to settle down for Diane. She didn't venture out of the house much, except to take Rocky for a walk on the beach each afternoon. There was no need to set a timer to remind her. Rocky seemed to know exactly the right moment to get her each day—just about the time she'd become so sleepy her head began to bobble like those dolls people stuck on their dashboards.

She was walking on the beach with him now. Well, she was walking—Rocky ran back and forth between her and the water's edge. She loved the fresh air and the chilling wind coming off the ocean. It was a tad colder now as they entered the second week of September, so she'd zipped her polar fleece jacket all the way up and, this time, she'd remembered to wear her Bogs.

Diane never tired of the view. On one end was the old Marble Cove Marina, surrounded by fishing boats, bait shops, and weathered wooden docks. Above those docks, gulls flew in and out, taunting each other like misbehaving children. She glanced northward, along the sand dunes and rocky beaches, which gradually climbed toward Orlean

Point and the lighthouse, the distinguished elder statesman of Marble Cove. It did seem like the perfect setting for a mystery novel.

She'd have to reread what she'd written. She didn't want to offend any of the locals when the book came out. They would undoubtedly wonder which of the characters in her book might be them, no matter how hard she'd try to disguise it. After all, every small town had a local newspaper, a coffee shop, a bookstore, a library, a grocery store. But if they didn't see themselves in the book, they'd imagine she was writing about someone else in town. Especially when she wrote about villains or town eccentrics.

She heard Rocky barking. He was chasing a group of seagulls, once again in vain. She glanced up at the lighthouse and then around its base. She realized she was actually hoping to spot the mysterious young man who'd been coming to town recently.

She wondered how Beverly was making out with her investigation into this new lead. She also wondered how Margaret's conversation with Allan had gone about the new giclée print idea. She knew that, with Allan's head for business, he'd immediately see the value of the project. But his pragmatic, accountant side would also see all the downsides and challenges. Not the least of which was someone having the kind of time it would take to pull it all together.

Diane would have loved to jump into something like that, especially having the chance to work with Margaret so closely. She could do all the research and become Margaret's adviser on the whole project. But of course she didn't have the time just now.

She wondered what Shelley had found out on her own little research project, looking into the necessary permits to start a baking business out of her home.

That reminded her—today the *Marble Cove Courier* came out with her classified ad inside. She looked at her watch. Maybe the paper had come while she'd been down here at the beach. Besides, she really needed to get back home to work on her proposal. *Work*, she thought. Was that really what her writing had been reduced to? Just work? A job?

No, she knew it was much more than that. She still loved writing and she loved this new opportunity God had given her. Her conflict was about the time issue. She hated having to choose between two things she loved to do.

"Rocky," she yelled. "C'mon, boy, time to head back." She turned and started walking the other way, knowing he'd be right behind her in a moment.

A section of a devotional she'd read just that morning floated up into her mind. The writer had talked about this very thing. The passage at the top was from Philippians 4:6, which said something like, "Don't worry about anything; instead, pray about everything." The devotional had suggested turning anxious thoughts into prayer reminders. That way, instead of their being wasted moments that brought her down, they'd become just the opposite: helpful thoughts that drew her closer to God.

So that's what Diane did. For the rest of her walk back to the house, she prayed for her friends and all these challenges they faced. As she turned into her walkway, she said a quick prayer for herself, asking God's help to bring all these ideas bouncing around in her head into something Frieda and her new publisher would love.

Before she opened the front door, she noticed something in Rocky's mouth. "Whatcha got there, Rocky?" Then she realized what it was. "The *Courier*! Good boy, Rocky." It was the last time the paper would print twice in a week until spring. Diane was glad she'd made the deadline to get her ad in this issue.

She opened the door and hurried inside, then sat on the sofa. "Bring it here." Rocky handed it to her, wagging his tail, then he sat down awaiting a pat on the head.

She pulled the paper from its plastic wrapper and spread it across the coffee table. Flipping through the pages, she scanned up and down for her ad. Finally, she found it:

COMPUTER HELP WANTED – Looking for someone with skill and experience in graphics and Web site design to put together a colorful brochure and Web site for a new home-based business. Good compensation, can work your own hours, but **needed immediately**. Please call.

Then below that, she'd written her phone number, also in bold print. She'd talked it over with Shelley and decided to put only her number in the ad. She didn't want to take the chance that someone might call Shelley's house during nap time.

Diane read the ad again and smiled. Not exactly her best work, but it would do. She was about to close the paper, but she read the ad one more time. *You are so silly,* she thought. After all this time, she still got a kick whenever she saw something she'd written in print. She could only imagine how it would feel to hold a copy of her first book.

She glanced at Rocky, who was sitting patiently by his empty water bowl. "I'm sorry," she said. "Let me get that for you." She got up and brought his bowl to the sink, deciding to make herself a cup of coffee before getting back to work. She'd just gotten the pot going when the doorbell rang. She opened it and saw Shelley standing there. Her expression told Diane that Shelley wasn't bringing good news.

"I guess God doesn't want me to do this baking thing," she said. "It's just one closed door after another."

"Come in, Shelley. I want to hear all about it. I've got coffee brewing. Would you like some?"

Shelley sighed. "That sounds nice."

"Come on in to the kitchen and have a seat. I want to hear all the details." Diane thought about cheering her up by showing her the ad in the *Courier,* but decided it might have the opposite effect. As Diane checked the coffeepot, Shelley began.

"It's really hopeless, Diane. I've been trying to stay positive about it, but I don't think we're going to find a silver lining in this batch of clouds."

"Is it really that bad?"

Shelley nodded. "The bottom line is that there's no way I can operate a baking business out of my home. I knew there was a problem before I even finished explaining the idea to the clerk at the town hall. His face was like granite."

"What'd he say?"

"Turns out there's all kinds of safety ordinances that come into play when you do anything commercial that involves cooking. Essentially, Dan and I would not just have to remodel our kitchen but, really, add a room to the back of the house big enough to fit all the commercial equipment we'd have to buy. We'd need to buy a commercial-grade oven, range, and refrigerator. We'd have to build a new heat and exhaust system and get a commercial-sized dishwasher. And if I wanted to fry anything, like doughnuts, we'd have to build a grease pit too."

"All of that just for a small home business?"

Shelley nodded. "They don't care *where* you do business or how big or small the operation is. Any commercial food-preparation operation has to have all these things. The clerk said, 'One size fits all.' All we can do from our home—without making all these changes—is bake things to give away at charity events or as gifts to friends."

"I'm so sorry, Shelley." Diane walked over to her and put an arm around her. "Do you have any idea how much all that would cost?" She didn't know why she'd asked that. Her instincts told her it would be way out of reach, even with her financial help.

"It's ridiculously expensive," Shelley said. "I stopped writing down the figures when I reached the ten thousand dollar mark. And that doesn't even begin to get at the remodeling costs. I talked it over with Dan, and he agreed. It's a deal breaker. Even if we could get the money somehow, he doubted we'd get permits to do something like that in our neighborhood."

"Did the clerk say that?"

"I didn't even ask," she said. "And, of course, renting a storefront downtown is completely out of the question with our budget. Besides that, the clerk mentioned he wasn't aware of any vacant ones that already had commercial kitchens."

It was all so sad. Surely something could be done.

"But it gets worse," Shelley said, tears now welling up in her eyes. "Dan is starting to think we might have to move out of Marble Cove now...for good. He was hoping that this idea would work, and we could limp along until it started to make decent money. Maybe between that and what he's still getting at the docks, we might have a chance. But now that they've cut his hours, we just can't keep going on like this." She wiped away the tears. "Oh, Diane, I don't want to move."

The poor thing. Diane got a sense that Shelley had come over here hoping against hope she might have some answers. But this time, Diane was all out of ideas. It was one thing to spend a few hundred dollars if someone had responded to the classified ad. But she didn't have the kind of money Shelley and Dan would need to move this mountain.

Diane walked over to the counter and grabbed a box of tissues. "Here," she said. "Surely there's some ground between 'made in the shade' and 'we have to move.' Have you thought about applying for a small-business loan? Or maybe even a grant? I've heard about angel investors who will put up seed money for businesses with real promise. You know, businesses like yours."

Shelley shook her head and blew her nose. "I just think it's over before it began!"

Diane squeezed Shelley more tightly in her hug. "You know, every one of us had our lives spared for a reason. God didn't do that just to lead us to disaster. Think of the miracles we've seen since then. Remember what He did for Margaret? She was all set to close down her gallery back in July. Then out of the blue she got the contract with the greeting card company. Don't give up hope yet."

"I want to believe that, Diane. I really do. But maybe this *is* His way of answering our prayers. Sometimes, like with my kids, they want something that's not good for them, and we have to say no."

"I know. That could be what's going on here." A verse of Scripture popped into Diane's head. "Okay, listen to this. It's from the Psalms, I can't remember which one, but it says God is our light and our salvation, so what do we have to fear? I'm going to pray that He'll be a light at the end of the tunnel for you and Dan. Because..." Now she was starting to choke up too. "I don't want you to move out of Marble Cove either."

CHAPTER ELEVEN

The following day, Margaret went in to the gallery an hour early, entering through the back door. It gave her some quiet time to paint and pray in peace, listen to some nice jazz, and think about the day ahead. Then at ten she'd turn the rest of the lights on in the gallery and unlock the front door. Sometimes customers would come in that first hour, but not often. Now that she had the greeting card contract, slow mornings were a gift.

As she set up the coffeepot and watered the plants, her heart was in turmoil from what Diane had told her yesterday evening about Shelley's situation. She wished there was something she could do. Shelley had her heart set on making a go of this baking business, and Margaret felt certain from the start that God had inspired the idea. Shelley was such a marvelous baker.

Margaret glanced over at her current painting on the easel and realized that Shelley was an artist too. If there was such a thing as the gift of baking, Shelley had it for sure. Margaret took some comfort in the fact that Shelley was young. If her dream didn't happen now, it still might come to pass later on. Margaret had waited until her sixties to see her dream realized.

More troublesome was the news that Dan and Shelley might have to leave Marble Cove. They hadn't been close for very long, but Margaret felt that God had brought Shelly, Diane, Beverly and her together this past summer in such a wonderful way. She was sure the four of them had a purpose, not just as individuals, but as a team. They were good friends who would become great friends in the days ahead.

But how would that be possible if Shelley moved away?

Margaret went back and fixed her coffee. She brought it over to the easel and set it down nearby. Margaret began working on her painting with fresh zeal, like the second wind a runner gets when he sees the finish line. She was getting so close to completing the work. She might even finish today, or certainly by tomorrow. It was turning out exactly the way she wanted.

It was hard to believe that in a few short months, this painting—her painting—would be seen by hundreds, even thousands, of people. And the other paintings that Matt Beauregard had taken—those would be seen even sooner on Lighting the Way greeting cards. It gave her a tremendous feeling of satisfaction. It wasn't about the money or any misguided notions of fame or recognition. It was about the blessing of seeing something that you've done, something you really put your heart into, being valued and appreciated by others.

She thought about the idea of rendering her paintings as giclée prints. Part of her recoiled from it, since she loved seeing her originals there on display. But, she realized with a shock, in a way, through these greeting cards, her paintings were already being made into prints. Now, instead of just one person at a time finding joy in her work, many others near and far would get that opportunity. And that thought made her genuinely happy.

She was so grateful that Diane had come up with this new idea. She marveled that she'd never thought of it before. She and Allan had actually bought a few art prints on a trip to Bar Harbor a few years back. She'd forgotten all about it. Sadly, she had never taken the time to get them framed. They sat rolled up in cardboard tubes in the back of her closet, right next to her shoes. One of these days, she'd have to get them out and make that happen. Of course, before that she'd have to free up some wall space at the house so she'd have somewhere to hang them.

She smiled as she remembered. They'd meant to take the prints to a framing shop, but Marble Cove didn't have one, and so they had stayed in their cardboard sleeves. *Come to think of it,* she thought, *Marble Cove needs a framer.* It was a shame that her prints hadn't seen the light of day.

After painting for just over an hour, she heard a banging on the back door, then muffled voices. It sounded like Allan and Adelaide. She opened it to find them carrying a coffee table Allan had made.

"Could you hold that door open, Margaret?"

"Sure," she said, standing aside. "Need a hand?"

"No, it's not heavy. Just awkward. Adelaide's doing just fine." He and Adelaide carried the table in. "Is that space up by the front window still open?"

"Yep," she said. "It's ready and waiting."

"You remember this one?" he asked as they walked by. "It replaces the one I shipped to that fellow in Vermont. He had some reason or another he couldn't wait, so I gave him the one in the store."

"I remember," Margaret said. "He wanted it for a wedding present for his daughter."

"That was it." They walked it to its place and set it down. Allan moved back toward the door. "I've got another piece to bring in, since you've got some extra room in here. Remember that fancy little storage box I've been making, the one folks put at the foot of their beds?"

"They call it a hope chest, Allan."

"That's the one. I finished it yesterday. Okay if I set it over there beside that mirror?"

Margaret looked to where he pointed. "That'll be fine, dear. I'm sure we'll sell some of those just as soon as people start to see it."

"Can I help?" Adelaide asked.

"Of course," Allan said. "I couldn't do it without you." She smiled and followed him out the back door.

In a few moments, Allan and Adelaide were back with the hope chest. They set it next to the mirror. Allan took a cloth out of his back pocket and wiped off his hands.

"Adelaide," Margaret said, "could you do me a favor and open the store, then watch things a few minutes while I talk to your father?"

"Sure, Mom. What do you want me to do?"

"Just greet anyone who comes in. And show them where the coffee is. Most people like to look around by themselves for a few minutes. We won't be long, but if they have any questions you can come get me."

Allan looked at her, his eyes almost asking a question.

"Nothing's wrong," she assured him. "I just want to tell you one thing and ask you about another." She walked back to the studio, and he followed. "Something you said about the extra space in here reminded me of something."

"You want to start charging me rent?" he said, smiling.

"No, it's nothing like that."

"Good, because I was thinking I might like to get a few more new pieces made in the next week or so. I'd bring them in before the fall fair. I think I could get some new orders with that kind of crowd in town."

"I'm sure you will," she said. "See, that's the thing I wanted to talk about … all the extra space in here. But before I do, I wanted to fill you in on some sad news Diane told me." She took a few minutes to brief him on how Shelley's baking business had suffered a setback and might even be falling through. She told him that the Bauers might have to move out of Marble Cove as a result.

His face registered concern. "I hope it doesn't come to that. I know Shelley moved here when they got married, but Dan's lived his whole life in Marble Cove."

"I don't suppose you need any help with your furniture orders?"

Allan shook his head. "Not really. I've got work, but not as much as the last time I hired Dan. It's really just enough for one man right now. Maybe after the fall fair, things might pick up to where I could hire him again. But I don't think it'd be enough work to make the kind of difference the Bauers would need. Maybe a day or two a week, at best. And that might just be for a few weeks. If they're thinking they might have to move, I'm afraid Dan needs something more permanent than I could offer."

Margaret leaned back against her desk. "That's what I thought. Let's remember to start praying for them. Now back to my first topic, about all the extra space in here. This has nothing to do with you putting your furniture on display. I'm happy to do that. It's about Diane's idea to start making giclée prints of all my paintings and to sell those to customers in addition to selling my original paintings. Have you had any more time to think that over?" Just then, she heard the bell ring out front, signifying that a customer had come in. She heard Adelaide give whoever it was her most cheerful greeting.

"I've thought about it some," he said. "On the surface, it seems like a nice idea."

There was a long pause. Margaret could tell he had a "but, you know" thought forming in his head.

"But, you know . . . it just doesn't seem like a good time to be doing something like that right now. You were hoping to get it going before the fall fair, right?"

Margaret glanced up at her wall calendar. "Not have it all together. But maybe just enough to where we could start telling customers about it. Maybe we could have some brochures printed up to pass out. Like you said, a lot of extra traffic will be coming through that weekend and—"

"Are you going to have time to do even that much between now and then?" he said. "With your greeting card deadlines?"

She knew she wouldn't.

"Would Diane?" he said.

"Not with her new book proposal project. I don't see how."

He straightened up, wiped his forehead with the shop towel hanging from his back pocket. "I'm not trying to shoot it down, Margaret. It's a good idea. Might just be the next logical phase for the gallery. But timing is one of the big challenges in growing a small business. Not just having new ideas, even good ones, but knowing the right time to develop them. I wish I could do it for you. My advice would be to get a little notepad and jot down all the things about this idea that pop into your head, so you don't lose them. Then we'll take another look at it after the dust settles from the fall fair."

"You're probably right," she said sadly. "I'll do that." She walked over to peek in on Adelaide.

"Well," he said, "I'll go fetch Adelaide up front and take her back to the house with me. I'll be fixing lunch in a little while. Want me to bring you some?"

"That would be nice." She saw Adelaide standing behind the counter. Adelaide smiled, waved, and pointed at two women standing in front of one of the paintings. Margaret followed Allan toward the front of the store and gave him and Adelaide a good-bye hug. They walked toward the back door. Before leaving, Adelaide gave her mother another nice smile and waved. She was such a joy.

Margaret walked over to the two women. "Can I get either of you ladies a cup of coffee?"

They both turned and smiled. One of the women was about Margaret's age and height but had darker hair. The other was a little younger and slightly taller. Margaret saw a resemblance and wondered if they might be sisters. "No, thank you," the shorter one said. "That young lady already offered it to us, but we've just come from the coffee shop next door."

"That's my daughter, Adelaide," Margaret said.

"We knew that," the other woman said. "She told us that right off. She's very proud of you, you know."

Margaret smiled, wondering what Adelaide had said.

"And she has every right to be," the younger of the two said. "You've got some lovely paintings here."

"See any you like in particular?" Margaret asked.

"That's the problem: I like all of the ones I've seen so far. Take this one here..." She turned and faced the painting in front of her. "I could reach right out and pick those blueberries," she said, pretending to do just that. "And the one right next to it, with the monarch butterflies. Absolutely gorgeous."

"Thank you. I'm glad you like them. Just take your time, and feel free to ask any questions." Margaret started to walk toward the counter.

"I did have one question." It was the older of the two women. "Actually, my sister was asking about this just before you came." She turned and spun slowly, taking in all the remaining paintings on the wall. "Are all these ... originals?"

"Yes," Margaret said.

"I thought so," she said. "That explains the price."

"I'm sorry that—"

"No, please. You don't need to apologize. For originals, they are remarkably low priced. It's just..."

"They are a little out of our reach," her sister said.

"I'm hoping to set up a new process to make giclée prints of them," Margaret said.

"I've heard of those! That means quality reproductions of the originals, right? On canvas?"

"Yes, that's right."

Their faces brightened. "Will that be anytime soon?"

"I hope so," Margaret said. "I certainly hope so."

CHAPTER TWELVE

It was such a lovely afternoon that Beverly decided to walk downtown, even though she'd already jogged two miles that morning. After her run, she'd removed the rest of the boxes from the hallway and living room, leaving just a small stack in her bedroom, safe from her father's curious eyes.

She had already put several boxes in the attic but didn't want to put these last few up there with them. They contained everyday items she knew she would use but that her father already had duplicates of. She wasn't sure how he'd react if she switched them out, especially since some of them had belonged to her mother. She decided she would exchange one or two over the next several days and see what happened.

Seeing her mother's things reminded Beverly of how much she missed her. A fresh wave of sorrow seemed to wash in just since she'd moved back to Marble Cove. Her mother had been gone for four years now, and Beverly thought she'd put most of her grieving behind her. These feelings seemed different from grief. More like a longing for her company and companionship and to hear her insights and responses to thoughts Beverly would share. To see her smile and to watch her wisdom at work. To learn from her as she cared for her father during this new phase of illness and aging.

Beverly hoped her mom would approve of the things she was doing.

She closed the front door, leaving her father resting comfortably in his library with a book. Mrs. Peabody was already at work in the kitchen, cleaning up the lunch dishes and getting ready to bake some surprise for dessert. She had to admit, Mrs. Peabody did have a way with her father. She wondered if it had anything to do with their similarity in age. Mrs. Peabody was at least a few years older than her father, but their gap wasn't that far apart. And Beverly got a kick out of the way she'd started calling him "the mister."

Even with his growing short-term memory loss, so far her father hadn't forgotten who Mrs. Peabody was, even once. He even seemed calmer whenever she was in the house. That by itself seemed reason enough to keep her on. But her cooking was undoubtedly the best reason. True, she could talk up a storm. And at times the sheer number of her words grated on Beverly. But it seemed a small price to pay compared to the benefits.

As she came out of her front yard onto the sidewalk, Beverly began to consider the mission ahead. She loved getting to play detective. She'd even made a photo of Orlean Point Light as the wallpaper on her laptop for inspiration. Her plan was to head into town and have a chat with August Jackson at the Cove. He'd invited her to meet at his house, but she knew that would turn a fifteen-minute talk into over an hour. After that, she would meet with Gerald Kimball at the *Courier*. Beverly wanted to see if she could pry loose any more information about this mysterious stranger. She'd already called Gerald, and he'd said he'd be at the paper all afternoon.

As she walked past Diane's house, she glanced over her shoulder at the lighthouse, thinking about some of the fresh memories it had generated over the summer. She and Diane weren't completely in sync about everything going on at the lighthouse and what it meant. Diane was convinced God was doing something supernatural, if not outright miraculous. Beverly certainly believed God *could* be involved in all this, but the growing body of evidence pointed toward a more human explanation. A man was getting inside the lighthouse, holding a flashlight or possibly a lantern.

Each month during the summer, they had inched a little closer to solving the mystery. At least, on the man-made side. And Diane had agreed with Beverly that this whole thing seemed like a wonderful plot for a novel. Not a murder mystery, thankfully, since no dead bodies were involved. But it had such an air of mystery about it, through and through. Beverly just had to find out what it was. She needed to find the pieces that would pull the puzzle together.

Somehow, she was sure this mysterious stranger would play a role.

★   ★   ★

When Beverly arrived at the Cove, she was happy to see the pastry cabinet almost bare. The few scattered items remaining on the racks did nothing to tempt her. She didn't need the extra calories. A quick glance around the room revealed she'd gotten there before August.

"What can I get for ya?" Brenna McTavish asked. "Sorry the pickin's are so slim on the baked goods."

"Not a problem, Brenna. I'll just have a cappuccino, medium."

"That's it?"

"This time."

"Coming right up."

When Beverly looked around again, she noticed the Cove was empty. It was probably just an odd hour. Then she remembered that it was September, and the downtown area was a lot quieter, especially on weekdays. "Brenna, I'm meeting August Jackson here in a few minutes. Do you know what he usually gets?"

"Oh yeah...Augie only orders coffee. No frills. Wants to have it in a mug too. 'The way coffee was meant to be drunk,' he says."

"Well, let me pay for his too. Do you know how he fixes it?"

"Sure do: cream only. I'll get you all set."

"Thanks."

After Brenna got their drinks together, Beverly paid her, dropped a nice tip in the jar, and headed for a table in the corner against the wall. Not two minutes later, Augie walked in.

"What do you say there, Brenna," he said. "Fine September afternoon, isn't it?"

"Sure is, Augie. Your date's over there in the corner. Already got your coffee just the way you like it. She even settled things up."

"Well, I'll be..." He walked over to Beverly. "Be still, my heart. Don't you look nice this afternoon, Mrs. Wheeland."

"Now, I'm not going to keep calling you Augie if you don't start calling me Beverly."

"I can do that, Beverly." He sat down and looked into his coffee mug. "Looks just right, Brenna. Thank you kindly."

"You're welcome, Augie. Not much in the pastry cabinet, but you're welcome to what's left. At this hour, I'll give it to you on the house."

"That's okay. Got some fresh blueberry-almond muffins waiting for me back at home." He leaned over and said quietly, "See what you could have had if we'd met at the house?"

"They sound delicious, but I need to get back and take care of my father. And I've got to stop at the *Courier* after here."

"I understand. How's he doing these days? Your father, I mean."

"About the same," Beverly said. "But his short-term memory is getting worse, I'm afraid. I don't like to leave him for very long."

"I'm surprised my old noggin's still sharp as it is, seeing how much older I am than he is. Can't take any credit for it, though. I think it's just in the genes." He took a sip of coffee. "Now that's a nice cup of coffee. Just can't bring myself to pay four dollars on all these fancy concoctions you young people drink these days. Lattes, cappuccinos, frappes, and the like."

Beverly took a sip of her "concoction," deciding not to mention that hers cost only $2.50.

"So what did you want to talk about, young lady? Let me guess, it's got something to do with Orlean Point, right?"

"Sort of," she said. "I know you talked with my friend Diane already."

"Nice lady. That's something, isn't it, about her book deal." He took another sip. "I wrote a novel myself once. Never got it published. Wasn't for lack of trying though. So I know how hard it is."

Beverly remembered the story and all about Augie's cookbooks. She decided to jump in quickly. "It's been a while since you talked with Diane, so I wondered if it had jogged your memory about the young man you told her about."

"You mean the one asking all those questions about the lighthouse?"

"That's the one. I'm particularly interested in the days he came into town."

"You mean which days of the week?" He sat forward in his chair.

"Yes. I know you said you didn't remember his name. But I really want to meet this man. I need to find out what he's, well . . . why he's so interested in the lighthouse, and what he knows about Edward Maker."

"So why do you want to know what days he came to town?"

"It's just an idea. But I thought if he came to town the same day each week, maybe I could come back on that day and meet him myself. Can you tell me what he looked like?"

"Come to think of it, he was quite a handsome fellow. About your age too, I'd say."

Beverly laughed. "Well, I'm not interested in meeting him *that* way."

"Oh well...let's see then." He scratched his chin. "What day did he come here? I didn't pay much attention to it, to be honest. Didn't know there'd be a quiz."

"I'm sorry," she said. "I know this must sound very strange. My friends and I have been trying to solve this mystery about the lighthouse, and we thought if—"

"I know you ladies love a good mystery."

"Yes, I guess we do. So, can you help me here?"

He sat back in his chair and scratched his head a few moments. "I'm sorry, Beverly. I just don't remember the day. He actually came to the library a few different days. Now, there's an idea. Have you stopped in there? Maybe he checked out some books. He was in there quite a while. You could ask them, see if he did. They'd have the dates in their computers, for sure."

"That might work," she said, but she instantly decided against it. She was pretty sure the library would have privacy policies against giving out that kind of information.

"Does this have something to do with that Maker fellow the young man was asking about?"

"I think it does. That's why we want to talk with him. Did Diane tell you about the inscription we found etched into the base of the lighthouse?"

"She did." He smiled. "The plot thickens."

Beverly took the last sip of her cappuccino. "I guess it must seem rather silly."

"Not in the least. I was a reporter way back when, remember? I love a good story."

Beverly stood up. "I'm sorry I can't stay longer."

"I understand. But you'll let old Augie know if you figure this mystery out, won't you?"

"I will, Augie. I promise. And thanks for meeting with me."

"Don't see that I helped any, but it was a pleasure. And like I told Diane, I'll keep my eye out. If I see that young man in town again, I'll let you know."

Beverly waved good-bye to Brenna and headed out the door. It was just a short walk to the *Courier* office. As soon as she walked in, she saw a tall man about her age behind the customer service counter.

"Mrs. Wheeland, I presume?" the man said, holding out his hand.

Beverly shook it and smiled. "And you must be Mr. Kimball. Please call me Beverly."

"Okay, Beverly. Then you call me Gerald."

"I suppose Abby is still on vacation?"

"She is. For a few more days anyway. Taking me a lot longer to get things done, working here at the office. I usually do all my writing at home. All the interruptions, I suppose."

"I'm sorry, Gerald. This shouldn't take but a few minutes."

"Oh, hey, I didn't mean that you're—"

"That's okay. Really."

"No, I'm talking about all the people coming in for the classifieds. Try as I might to make it self-serve, they still all feel the need to get me involved. But you...you are a welcome intrusion."

If Beverly discerned correctly, he said this with a certain gleam in his eye. She definitely didn't want to give Gerald that kind of impression. "Well, thank you," she said. "But I'll be out of your hair in a few minutes." She didn't mean to, but she looked up and noticed he was mostly bald. She quickly looked away, but she thought he noticed.

"You mentioned on the phone about wanting to know more about the man who's been coming into town lately, asking about Orlean Point Light."

"I did."

"Something about which days he was here."

"I know you told Diane you weren't here then. I was just wondering if you had some kind of logbook you ask people to sign when they go upstairs to the morgue. I don't remember signing one when Diane and I were here a while back."

"No, we don't. Truth is, hardly anyone ever goes up there." His eyes drifted toward the stairway. "If we had a logbook somewhere, I've never seen it."

That was disappointing. It seemed like Beverly was just wasting her time, and everyone else's.

"But have no fear, Gerald Kimball is here. I texted Abby after your call, and she called me back about twenty minutes ago. I think we're in luck."

"We are?"

He nodded, all smiles. "Abby said she got a little suspicious when he came in the second time. But it really stuck with her when he came in a third time, just a few days later. It wasn't the way he looked, mind you. It just seemed odd to her, an out-of-towner taking such an interest in Orlean Point Light. She didn't remember his name, and she didn't want him to think she didn't trust him, since he seemed like such a nice fellow. But she did scratch down a few notes, just in case something went missing upstairs later on."

"She did?"

"Sure did. She told me where that note might be. Took a while, but I found it." He looked down and fumbled through some papers. "Here it is. She didn't write down very much. She just jotted down the three days he visited. She told me she was going to try to find out his name if he came in again. But he hasn't, and then she went on vacation. I wrote the dates on this Post-it note for you."

"You did? Gerald, that's wonderful!"

"I thought you might like it."

He was giving her that look again. She took the paper. "I really owe you one, Gerald. Thank you so much."

"Well, I can think of a way you can—"

"I've really got to get home to take care of my father. Thanks again, Gerald." She offered her hand. He shook it, and she hurried out the door.

Chapter Thirteen

As Beverly turned the corner onto Newport Avenue, she saw Diane doing a little weeding in the flower beds under her front window. *Perfect,* she thought. She had already stopped by the gallery before leaving the downtown area and filled Margaret in on the news. After talking to Diane, she'd cross the street and update Shelley.

Standing on the sidewalk, Beverly called out, "When you're done there, you can start work on the beds at my house."

Diane looked up and wiped her forehead with a gloved hand. Then she straightened up and worked out a kink in her back. "I think I can safely say yes to that," she said, "seeing as I'll never be done here."

Beverly laughed and walked down Diane's herringbone brick walkway. "Are you getting a little ahead on your book proposal?"

"No, I just needed to take a break and get some fresh air. I was going to walk on the beach, but the last several days when I'd get home..." She looked down. "I'd walk right by these beds. Each time I did, it was like they were sticking their tongues out at me."

Beverly smiled and shook her head. "You do have a way with words."

"You don't look dressed for a run. Did you just come from town?"

"I did, and I have some neat things to share with you. I already filled Margaret in." She looked over at the two white Shaker rockers on her porch. "Mind if I sit in one of those?"

"No, and I'll join you." She stood. "My back could use a break. Do you want a cup of coffee or a bottle of water?"

"I'm fine. I just came from the Cove."

Diane stepped up on the porch and sat down. "So...what did you find out?"

Beverly sat forward and held out Gerald's little Post-it note. "Here are the days and times our mystery man visited the *Courier*."

Diane took it and looked at it a moment. "*Hmm*, good work. But I don't see how this helps us find out who he is."

"Well, I've studied it, and it appears he comes on Thursday afternoons and Saturday mornings. Maybe those are his days off. I was thinking, among the four of us, we could do a little stakeout on those times, and one of us is bound to catch him. You know, like the stakeout we did at the lighthouse before."

Diane stopped rocking. "But what are we supposed to do, have one of us sit outside the *Courier* and another by the library? For hours at a time?"

"That's what I was thinking at first. Then I realized there was no way you and Margaret could do that, not with your deadlines. But I had an idea. When I was at the library, I noticed a certain table by the front window. It's at just the right angle. When you sit there, you can actually look down the street and see the front door to the *Courier.* So only one of us has to be there at a time. If you sit at that table, you can watch both places. You could work on your laptop there, couldn't you? I figured that we could each take one two-hour shift, some on Thursday and the others on Saturday morning." She waited a moment. "So what do you think?"

"I guess that could work. I suppose I could take the second two-hour slot on Saturday mornings."

Beverly stepped out of the rocker. "Margaret said she could do the early shift on Saturdays between nine and eleven. I'll go see if Shelley can take a slot. And I'll pick the last empty one. And really, Diane, if you can't do your slot, just tell me. I'm working from home now, so I can pick my own hours. I know you're really pressed for time."

"Well, thanks for that grace. But I can't see how doing something two hours a week could be too hard. Like now, I need a good diversion every so often or I'll go stir crazy. And I can still work from there."

"So you'll take the second shift on Saturday mornings?"

"I'd be happy to. So, do we know any more about what he looks like?"

"Not much," Beverly said, stepping off the porch. "I started to ask Augie, but he got the wrong idea. He started telling me how handsome he was." Diane laughed. "He did mention that he's about my age and has dark hair. I'm thinking that, this time of year, there aren't too many folks in town 'from away,' as folks around here say. It should be easy to spot a stranger."

"Well, that's great, Beverly. Good job." Diane got up from her rocker. "The plot thickens."

"That's the same thing Augie said." Beverly took a few steps toward the sidewalk. "Do you know if Shelley is home?"

"I'm pretty sure she is," Diane said. "Though I haven't seen her this afternoon. Oh, that reminds me—you probably haven't heard."

"Haven't heard what?" She stopped and turned around.

"About Shelley's baking business maybe falling through."

"Oh no."

"It gets worse." Diane's face instantly became sad. "She and Dan might have to move out of Marble Cove. His work at the docks seems to be drying up, and now with this baking thing looking like it's falling apart . . . well, I'll let her tell you. It depresses me to even think about it."

"That's terrible. But surely it can't be that bad. There's got to be something we can do."

"The only thing I can think of is to pray."

$$\star \quad \star \quad \star$$

Three hours later, Beverly was back at Shelley's front door. She'd stopped by after visiting Diane, but the Bauers had been eating an early dinner. Since Dan had gotten home from the docks shortly after one in the afternoon, there'd been no reason to wait until the normal dinner hour, Shelley had said. She told Beverly that if she came back at this time, Shelley would have the kids down for the night, and they could talk.

She'd looked so sad.

Beverly had thought perhaps she should drop this little stakeout project, or at least not try to involve Shelley. But she decided to tell her anyway. She knew how much Shelley enjoyed this whole lighthouse mystery. Maybe she'd find it a pleasant distraction. She hoped they weren't planning to move right away. She also wished she hadn't thrown out all those boxes now. Maybe Shelley could have used them. The door suddenly opened.

It was Shelley. "Are you going to knock or just stand there? I thought I heard someone outside and saw you through the curtains."

"Yes, I'm sorry. I was just thinking about you. Is this a good time?"

"Sure, come in. The kids are all bathed and in bed. Dan's watching TV. We can talk at the table. I'll put some coffee on."

"I'd love some." She noticed that Shelley was talking quietly, so she did the same. She walked through the living area and said a quiet hello to Dan, who was watching a baseball game on TV.

"You have some news about our little lighthouse mystery?" Shelley asked as she poured the coffee.

"I do, but Shelley, I want you to know how sorry I am about the setback to your baking business. Diane told me. She also told me about the possibility you might have to move away." Shelley's face clouded as she walked the mugs to the table. "But listen, we don't have to talk about it, if you don't want to. I know what it's like to be working through something depressing, especially something you have no control over. Sometimes you want to talk about it, and sometimes it's the last thing you want to do."

"Thanks, Beverly." Shelley sat down and began fixing her coffee. "At the moment, I'm trusting God and doing okay. Ask me again an hour from now."

Beverly smiled. She knew exactly what Shelley meant.

"Dan and I went over our finances. It looks like we can hobble along here for a few more weeks, but not much longer than that. We talked about him trying to get work on one of the fishing boats...for about ten minutes."

"That's dangerous work," Beverly said. "Until I saw one of those shows on the Discovery Channel, I had no idea."

"That, and they go out for weeks at a time. Sometimes a month or more."

"So what's he going to do?"

"He's going to start looking for work on the Internet. Maybe he'll drive into the bigger towns, like Portland and Bangor, on the weekends to see if they have more work. If he finds something, he'll take it and commute. Until winter sets in. Maybe by then, we'll have sold the house." She sighed, then sipped her coffee. "But tell me about your lighthouse news."

Over the next ten minutes, Beverly told her everything.

Shelley's face lit up the more Beverly talked. Shelley totally loved the stakeout idea. "But with Dan being gone on the weekends," she said, "I can probably only do the Thursday slot."

"That's no problem. Which one would you prefer?"

"Better do the later of the two. There's a better chance Dan will be home from work then, and the kids will be down for their naps. But there could be a glitch. If he does have work for the whole day, I won't have anyone to watch the kids."

"Don't worry about it. Just call my cell phone if that happens, and I'll do both shifts on Thursday."

"But the way it's been going," Shelley said, "Dan will be home."

"Do you think you can start this Thursday?"

"Sure, I don't see why not."

"Then it's settled. We'll start this w—"

"He was *out,* you knucklehead!" Dan yelled at the TV. "Are you blind?"

Both women looked in the direction of the living room.

"Dan?" Shelley said. "The kids."

"Oh, sorry."

Beverly turned and looked at Shelley. "Do you mind telling me a little about what happened with the bakery idea? Did it have anything to do with Diane not being able to do the brochures and Web site?"

"Some, I guess."

"I saw the ad in the *Courier*, by the way," Beverly said. "Any bites yet?"

"No, not a single one."

"Well, I was thinking. I have some experience doing both of those things from my job. And now that I'm working at home, I can choose my own hours. I'm sure I could work on getting both of those things done for you."

"Really? That's so kind of you to offer, but—"

"I might even be able to get a good bit of it done in time for the fall fair. Wasn't that your goal, to have something ready to pass out to people at the fair? You'd have to help some, like bake samples of the things you'd want to sell so we can take a bunch of pictures. But the best part is that I wouldn't have to charge you a penny. And I know of some really inexpensive Web design software we can get off the Internet. I've used it before. It's not very sophisticated, but we can make it look pretty professional. Maybe later, after your business is doing well, you can hire someone to make it really nice."

But the look on Shelley's face wasn't what Beverly had expected. If anything, she looked sadder. "I'm sorry. Listen to me, rattling on like that."

"No, that's a wonderful idea, Beverly. I'd love it if you could do all that, but that only solves a part of our problem." She reached over for a napkin and dabbed her eyes. "The biggest obstacle is something neither you nor anyone else can help us with." She went on to describe the permit problem with the city, explaining how they'd have to completely remodel the house to meet all the safety regulations for a commercial kitchen. It was either that, or rent a storefront downtown to bake in. She and Dan didn't have money to even consider doing either one.

The more she talked, the more Beverly realized how hopeless the situation really sounded. What good would it do to have stacks of full-colored brochures printed up, or even a fabulous Web site highlighting all the wonderful desserts Shelley could make, if she didn't have a kitchen to bake in?

CHAPTER FOURTEEN

The following Thursday came and went with no signs of the mysterious stranger. It was now midmorning on Saturday. The second shift, so to speak. Diane was just about to enter the library to relieve Margaret so she could get over and open the gallery.

She saw Margaret sitting at the assigned post: a little table by the front window. She tucked her laptop case under her arm and headed toward her.

It was a quaint old library. It was on the small side, exactly what you'd expect to find in a town the size of Marble Cove. It had tight little rows and hardwood oak tables with chairs tucked in here and there. The furniture was all very square and plain, and Diane was pretty sure the entire collection was older than she was. Of course, Diane loved libraries. As a reporter who'd spent the first half of her career digging up story details before the era of computers and the Internet, she'd logged in countless hours in libraries.

Alas, when she did research for her novels now, almost everything she needed was only a few clicks away on her computer. Still, on occasion, she'd discover that an answer to some question was located only in an out-of-print book not available on the Internet. That would give her a happy excuse to get out of the house and come down here to the library. That was where an older library like the one here in Marble Cove really paid off. They had hundreds of out-of-print books.

When she got to the table where Margaret sat, Margaret was slowly flipping the pages of a big coffee table book about lighthouses, looking up every few moments to glance out the window toward the front door of the *Courier* office.

"By the expression on your face, I'm guessing you haven't seen any mysterious strangers either."

Margaret looked up, somewhat startled. "Oh, Diane, it's you." She smiled. "No, not a sign. I've seen a few women head into the *Courier,* probably to place ads. And I saw a nice out-of-town couple stroll by, but they walked right by the *Courier.*"

"I half expected to find you with a pair of binoculars," Diane said.

"Like they do stakeouts in movies," Margaret said. "I know, or maybe a camera with a telephoto lens. I'm hoping to look inconspicuous sitting here. I'd die if the librarian came over and asked me what I was doing."

Diane sat down. "Just say you're on a stakeout."

Margaret laughed. "Wouldn't that be a scream in a town like Marble Cove? What if people got wind of what we're up to? Detective Little already thinks we're loony. I suppose Gerald and Augie might agree with him at this point."

"I don't know," Diane said. "They're both reporters. Good reporters are always a little suspicious and love a good story."

Margaret stood up. "How are things coming on your book proposal?"

"Actually, since things have quieted down the last several days, it feels like I'm finally making some progress. Some ideas are starting to gel. I'm making a lot of good notes. But I'm still in the brainstorming stage. How about you? How are things going with your lighthouse paintings?"

"Oh, that's right, you don't know. I've got a big surprise to show you. Can you stop off at the gallery before you head home this afternoon?"

"Sure. But are you going to leave me in suspense until then?"

"I hate to, but I really want you to see it when I tell you."

"See it?"

Margaret nodded. "You'll understand when I show it to you. But to answer your question, I finished that first painting a few days ago, and I'm already working on the second."

"Does the surprise have anything to do with the giclée prints idea?"

Margaret sighed and said, "No, I'm afraid not. I guess we haven't talked for a few days. Allan and I discussed it. I loved the idea, and he seems to be...warming up to it. He even said he thinks we should probably do it. It's just not the right time. I've got to stay focused on the greeting card paintings, and Allan's furniture business is picking up some steam."

She began gathering her things together. "He's trying to get a few new pieces built to display at the fall fair. He can't pursue the giclée project right now, and I sure can't. *You* can't do it. But I do have some hope now that it's actually going to happen. I've even begun to talk about it with my customers. Especially the ones who leave disappointed because they don't have the money to buy an original."

"Are you getting their names down? And e-mail addresses?"

"No."

"Oh, you should."

"Isn't that being a little pushy?" Margaret slid her chair under the table.

"Not if they already like your paintings. I'll bet they'd love to know when they'll finally become available as prints. Hey...wait a minute."

Someone caught Diane's eye, a man walking toward the *Courier* office. His back faced them, so they couldn't see his face. She stood up to get a better look.

Margaret looked too. "That can't be him," she said. "He looks too old. My eyes aren't great, but isn't that gray hair on his head?"

"You're right. It's not him. Beverly said he had dark hair and that he was about her age."

"And good-looking, I take it."

Diane laughed as she looked away. "It's always better when a mysterious stranger is good-looking and has dark hair." She sat back in her chair again.

"Well, I better go open up the gallery." Margaret walked toward the door.

"Get yourself a nice clipboard to put by the register," Diane said. "Be bold. If someone shows interest in a painting, and you find out they can't afford it, just ask them if they'd like to be notified when prints become available."

"I suppose I can do that."

"Of course you can, Margaret. If I were in their shoes, I wouldn't think twice about giving you my name and e-mail address."

"Okay, I'll do it." When she reached the door, she turned. "Don't forget to stop by later on."

"I definitely will."

★   ★   ★

Diane slid the book from the shelf. This was a book she'd been hoping to find for weeks. Someone from her online writer's group had recommended it, though she said it was almost impossible to find. She blew the dust off and opened to the title page. It was written in 1937. It was a book all about poisons and antidotes discovered by a medical doctor who'd journeyed deep into the jungles of Africa. Finding this was like discovering gold for a mystery writer. The pages were yellow and stiff, and the binding was slightly torn.

She had hoped to make copies of specific pages, but she didn't dare risk damaging it further. She walked it back to the table by the window, deciding she'd have to make some notes on her laptop instead.

With this find, she decided her two hours at the library would not be a total waste of time after all. No dark-haired, handsome strangers had walked into the *Courier* or into the library. Diane knew everyone she'd observed in that span of time, by sight if not by name.

She sat there studying the book thirty minutes more, then got up, put it on the reshelving cart, and headed out the door.

It was a little past one, but she had eaten a late breakfast before coming to the library, so she wasn't quite ready for lunch. She decided to stop in at the Cove and work a few more hours on her book proposal. Then she'd visit Margaret at the gallery to find out about this big surprise. A nice latte would be just the thing to help her get in a writing mood. That, and maybe a small snack from the pastry cabinet. She had to keep her blood sugar up, of course.

When she walked in, Brenna McTavish was busy rinsing something at the sink in the back corner. Diane said hi, but Brenna seemed not to have heard her. She stepped back and began to examine the pastries. She couldn't help noticing that the cabinet was almost empty. *They must have had a busy morning,* she thought. She lifted an almond biscotti from a big jar on the counter. It would have to suffice.

"Hey, Diane, good to see you. What can I get for you?"

"What I always get, Brenna. And let's throw in this biscotti." Diane set it next to the register. "Had a busy morning?"

Brenna had already started on her latte. "About average for a Saturday morning, I suppose." She shrugged. "Say, have you seen the paper yet? Someone we both know and love is smack-dab on the front cover."

"Really? I haven't seen it yet. You have a copy?"

"There's one sitting right over there on that empty table by the window."

Diane gripped her laptop case and walked over. *How wonderful!* she thought. Of course, she knew this was going to ruin Margaret's big surprise. This had to be what she wanted to show Diane. The headline of the *Marble Cove Courier* read "Marble Cove Artist Gets Major Deal!"

Her first thought was, "Really, Gerald, is that the best headline you could come up with?" But her second thought quickly washed that one away. Because there, under the headline, was a picture of her good friend Margaret, a big smile on her face, proudly standing next to her first new painting for Lighting the Way.

"Ain't that something?" Brenna said. "I knew Margaret was a good painter. You could see that just walking by her gallery. But I didn't know about this big deal she got with them greeting card folks."

"It really is something," Diane said. "They're using several of her paintings, and they've asked her to do some new ones just for them."

"I know," Brenna said. "The article tells all about it. Here's your latte."

Diane paid her. "I'm going to take this over to my usual table over there by the window. Can't wait to read it. Will it be okay if I work here for a few hours, since you're not too busy?"

"Sure. Stay as long as you like. But remember, we're closing at five now. We do that after Labor Day, until the spring."

"I'll be out of your way before then." Diane walked over to her table, set her coffee and biscotti down, and laid her laptop on the seat. For the next several minutes, she read Gerald's article about Margaret's "major deal." Gerald might not have hit it out of the park with his headline, but he'd written the article very well. It was an above-average human interest piece. He'd treated Margaret's accomplishments with all the honor she deserved.

He'd even contacted Matt Beauregard, the CEO of Lighting the Way, for a quote. Matt told all about the story of how, back in the summer, he and his daughter had ducked into the Shearwater Gallery to find shelter from a storm. He said that he now looked back at that moment as providence from God. He went on and on about how beautiful Margaret's paintings were and how he couldn't stop thinking about them for several days. And now he was sharing her gift with all their customers throughout New England.

Oh, good, Diane thought, as she read the last paragraph. Gerald quoted Margaret talking about her plans to begin making giclée prints of her paintings soon. Then he explained what they were, and how these prints would make "these breathtaking scenes" available at more affordable prices. He invited everyone in Marble Cove to stop by the gallery and see all this for themselves.

"That should do great things for Margaret's business, don't you think?" Brenna said.

"Yes," Diane said. "This is wonderful. Do you mind if I keep this one? I get it at the house, but I think I might stop by the *Courier* and get a bunch more."

"Feel free," Brenna said. "I got another copy here behind the counter."

Diane closed the paper over, folded it, and put it by her laptop case. She pulled her laptop out to start working on her proposal. As she opened up her document, she prayed, *Thank You, Lord, for blessing my good friend this way.* Then she added a quick prayer for Shelley, asking that God would light the way for her and Dan, so that somehow they might not have to leave Marble Cove.

CHAPTER FIFTEEN

Shelley was trying to keep her heart in a place of faith about this, but it felt like an uphill climb on a slippery slope. She had hoped Dan wouldn't leave to start looking for work for at least another week. "You sure you have to go?" she asked as he walked past her in the hallway, dragging a small rollaway suitcase. A suitcase she had just helped him pack.

Dan let go of the suitcase and came back. She tensed, expecting a harsh reaction. Instead, he reached for her left hand and lifted her chin gently with the other. "Look at me, Shelley," he said softly. She looked up into his eyes and saw love and concern, not the old defensive glare she expected to find. "I thought I could wait another week too. But I can't stand just sitting here waiting for something to happen. I'd rather be out searching, you know?"

She pulled him into a hug and rested her head against his strong shoulders. "I know."

"Maybe you can keep looking for some way we could stay here in Marble Cove," he said. "Maybe we could stay but live in a small apartment somewhere or something. But our savings are almost gone, and each week my paychecks are getting smaller. I have to try to find work."

"I know. But do you have to stay gone overnight?" She realized that the ache in her heart wasn't just about moving anymore. She was going to miss Dan and miss him being in the house. Through this trial, God had brought them closer together. Even here, this was not how the "old Dan" would have handled her struggle. "I don't want you to leave," she said. "I'll miss you."

"I'll miss you too, Daddy."

They both looked down. Aiden had gotten up from his nap. He had his arms wrapped around Dan's leg. "Where are you going?"

Dan bent down so he could talk face-to-face. "Remember what I said before your nap, Aiden? I won't be gone long. Just tonight and part of tomorrow. I'll be back tomorrow night, maybe even before your bedtime."

"Is that all?" he said.

Shelley had to restrain herself. He said it so sweetly, and she knew he had no idea how long Dan would actually be gone. He was at that age where the concept of time was a complete muddle.

"That's all," Dan said. "I'll be home before you know it. Here, let me give you another good-bye hug." He picked Aiden up and gave him a big squeeze, just as he had done before Aiden's nap. "Can you go watch a video for a few minutes so I can talk to your mom?"

"Sure." He ran off, happy as ever.

Dan faced Shelley and put his hands on her shoulders. "Speaking of videos," he said, "do you know what this is like,

Shelley? Remember, before the kids were born, I bought you that whole set of *Little House on the Prairie* videos?"

She nodded. "And we watched them together on the couch."

"For hours and hours," he said.

"I thought you liked them. You made me promise not to tell your brothers that we watched it."

"And you never will." He said it, faking a threatening tone. She smiled. "I did like them. Mostly, I liked being with you on the couch. It took a while, but I definitely got into the stories. I just remembered one. Remember that time when things weren't going too well at the Ingalls farm? The crops didn't come in, or some other thing."

"Yes."

"And Charles had to leave for a few months to go find work in the city. He went off with that friend of his, the big guy with the dark hair and beard."

"Isaiah."

"That's the guy."

"But Charles was gone for months."

"See, I'm not going anywhere near that long. Just one day."

"But if you get the job, you'll be gone all week long for a while."

"Right, but not for two weeks. And even then I'll still get to come home on the weekends. Charles didn't get to come home that often. And when I leave you and the kids, I'm leaving you with indoor plumbing and electricity."

She laughed.

"That's what I want to see. Now, I need to head out to see what my uncle has in mind."

Shelley didn't let go. "Do you really think you should work with your uncle? I mean, I know we prayed and then your uncle called, so maybe I should see it as an answer to our prayers. But I don't like you leaving."

Word of their money troubles had spread to Dan's extended family, including the fact that Dan might have to start looking for work outside of Marble Cove. Dan's uncle Mike lived near Portland, Maine. He'd called saying he might have something for him. His friend was a painting contractor who'd just gotten a big contract. Some solid work for a couple of months. He said he needed at least two or three new guys.

Uncle Mike had called asking if Dan wanted him to put in a good word for him. He said he'd probably get the job just on his say-so. Dan and Shelley had had that difficult conversation just over two hours ago. When Dan called back, Uncle Mike had suggested Dan come there now and stay the night. He could set up the interview for Sunday afternoon.

"Maybe it is God answering our prayers," Shelley said, "but it all seems so rushed. And if you go there now, you'll miss church in the morning. Can't you just leave after church tomorrow?"

"I'm actually leaving now so I *can* make it to church in the morning. I'll go with Uncle Mike's family. He said this contractor could only meet me between one and two thirty tomorrow. We're having lunch at some barbeque place. If I left from here after church, I'd never make it there on time. And it's not really such a rush, if you think about it. The interview is tomorrow, but Uncle Mike said the work doesn't start for another two weeks. See, we'll have plenty of time to get used to the idea before it starts."

She knew there was no use pushing this, and he was being so nice about it. She didn't want to get him upset, especially since he was about to leave town.

He kissed the top of her head. "I'll be there and back before you know it." He grabbed the suitcase handle and led her down the hallway by the hand. They walked outside and closed the front door quietly, trying not to disturb Aiden or send Prize into a barking fit.

Shelley stood there on the walkway as he opened the truck and put the suitcase behind the front seat. "Do you want me to talk to Patricia Finley tomorrow about putting the house up for sale? I'll probably see her at church."

He turned around, a pained expression on his face. He looked at the house from one side to the other. "I don't know if I'm ready for that."

"But your Uncle Mike said you're a shoo-in to get the job. And I know this guy is going to like you five minutes into the conversation at lunch tomorrow. So I'm just looking down the road a little. The job may not start for two weeks but, once it does, you'll be there all week every week for at least a few months. I just thought that maybe we should have Patricia over the first part of the week, while you're still in town. That way, if she sees anything we need to fix to get the house ready to sell, you can get it done before the painting job starts."

Dan sighed loudly. "No, that's good, hon. You're thinking more clearly than I am. It's just…it's such a big step, calling the Realtor. Makes it feel…"

"Like it's really gonna happen?" Shelley said.

He nodded, then looked down at the ground. "Yeah, I guess you better talk to her. I hope she doesn't find too much wrong with it. I'd hate to have to spend my last two weeks here doing fix-it projects."

She walked over and put her arms around his waist. "We could do them together."

"I know," he said.

But she knew what he meant. And this surfaced another fear she had, about how much they'd get selling the house with the economy the way it was. They hadn't lived in it that many years. She wasn't sure if they even had any equity built up yet. They might even wind up owing a little more than they'd get in a sale. If they even could get a buyer. "You have any idea what our house is worth?" she said. "In case Patricia asks me what we'd hope to get for it?"

"No. I haven't started looking into it yet. I guess I've been in denial. I thought I had at least a few more weeks. It's a lousy time to be selling a house."

"Do you think we might have to live in an apartment…*if* we move?" She said *if,* but she felt like saying *when* we move. Seemed like a foregone conclusion at this point.

"Maybe, but let's don't go there now. That really does feel like rushing it."

"I mean, if we move to an apartment, we'd probably have to find a new home for Prize." The thought saddened Shelley more than she would have expected. Prize now seemed like a part of the family. "The kids will take that pretty hard."

"Apartments aren't all bad." Dan looked over at the garage. "But I'd lose my workshop too. I didn't think about that. What am I going to do with all my tools in an apartment?" He shook his head. "Well, I can't think about all this stuff now."

"I'm sorry. I shouldn't have brought it up."

"That's okay. We'll need to face all this eventually."

"And," she said, trying to inject some hope that she didn't actually feel at the moment, "if this is God's way of answering our prayers, He'll take care of all these big unknowns."

Dan nodded sadly. "Man, I hate this."

* * *

Diane looked at her watch. She needed to wrap this up. The Cove was closing in fifteen minutes. But it really had been a fruitful afternoon of writing, even if the stakeout that morning had been a complete bust.

It was becoming clear to Diane that, instead of trying to come up with two brand-new mysteries for her main character to solve, she should adapt two other mystery stories she'd roughed out last year. It would take some work to make them fit, but it was a whole lot less work than creating two brand-new stories from scratch.

She looked around and noticed she was the only customer left in the restaurant. When she looked up at Brenna, she was standing behind the counter looking at her.

"Good," Brenna said. "I was just about to take the broom to ya." She was smiling.

"I'm sorry," Diane said. "I told you I'd be out of here way before you closed. I guess I got lost in my writing." She shut her laptop and stood up to emphasize that she really was getting ready to go.

Brenna walked over to the front door and flipped the sign over, announcing they were closed. "I know it's still a few minutes before five," she said, "but I don't want any last-minute customers popping in, not after I've already got everything cleaned up for the evening."

Diane gathered her things together and walked toward the front door. Brenna walked back behind the counter. "Say," she said, "want to take any of these baked goods home with you? There's just a few left. The owners don't want me to keep them overnight. It's bad enough that they're store-bought. I don't want to serve them stale the next day."

"Well, let me see what you've got left." She walked over to the pastry cabinet. There really wasn't much. She didn't see a single thing she'd ever ordered before. "I had no idea these pastries were store-bought."

"These ones are," Brenna said. "And the stuff I've been putting in there the last few days. But not as a rule. You probably never met our baker, Freddy. No, the stuff you're used to getting is stuff he baked fresh every day."

"I didn't think they all could have been store-bought. They were always so delicious and fresh."

"That's because they were. Freddy was really talented."

"What happened to him?"

"Nothing. He's been in the Army Reserve the last few years, and then he decided he wanted to be a soldier full-time. Two days ago, he shipped out."

"Really?" Diane said. "And how long will he be gone?"

"I don't know," Brenna said. "A few years anyway."

"And you haven't been able to find anyone to take his place?"

"Nope. I know they weren't looking to pay someone a lot of money. I'm guessing that was the problem. Freddy did all right because he was single, still lived at home. You know those franchise coffee shops hire out. None of their stuff is baked right there in the store."

"I kind of figured that," Diane said. "The pastries here were always much better than I ever got at one of those places."

"And way better than this store-bought stuff," she said. "So, you want some?"

"How about if I take those three cinnamon twists on the bottom shelf off your hands?"

"That's it? How about these...what are they...guess they're apple fritters?"

"No, just the cinnamon twists." As she watched Brenna work, an incredible idea began forming in her head. "Brenna, will you be talking to the owners anytime soon?"

"Usually talk to them every day. Why?"

It might just work, she thought. "I'm not sure, but...I have an idea they might want to hear."

"Really, what about?"

"Your bakery problem. I might just have a solution that would solve your problem and a *big* problem for a good friend of mine."

CHAPTER SIXTEEN

Diane was almost beside herself with joy. It was perfect. Brenna McTavish stood there on the other side of the pastry cabinet, a puzzled look on her face. "So let me get this straight," Diane said. "You have a full commercial kitchen back there with all the right permits to bake all the pastries you've been serving in this cabinet."

"That's one way to put it," Brenna said. "Up until the last few days anyway, before Freddy shipped out."

"And you've been trying—well, the owners have—but can't find anyone in town to hire as a baker?"

Brenna nodded.

"And you're closing the Cove at five every day, from now until spring, right? Do you know the owners pretty well?"

"I guess. Been working for them several years. So what's this all about, Diane? You gonna keep me in suspense?"

"Brenna, I think I've found your new baker, and it may not cost them a dime to hire her."

"Her?" she said. "Do I know this person?"

"You do, but I'd need to call her first to make sure she'd want to do this. Although I can't imagine her saying no. Can you just wait a few minutes so I can call her?"

Brenna looked at the clock on the wall. "Sure. If it'll put an end to me having to put out this store-bought stuff anymore, I'm all for it."

"Well, I'll just step outside, if that's okay, and call her. Is the door locked?"

"Not yet."

"I'll be right back." Diane walked outside, pulled out her cell phone, and speed-dialed Shelley's number.

"Hello, Diane." Shelley's voice sounded weary over the phone. "Perfect timing. Dan just left about ten minutes ago. I could use some cheering up."

"He did? Where did he go?"

"He's driving to Portland. His uncle's house. He called with a job offer. One of his friends is a painting contractor, and he's got some big job starting in two weeks. His uncle said he's a shoo-in to get it, but he needed to get down there tonight so he can interview with the man after church tomorrow."

"Well, after you hear what I have to say, you might want to call Dan and tell him to turn that pickup around."

"What?"

"Do you remember that small miracle we've all been praying for? I think it's here."

"What? Diane, what are you saying? Tell me." She was getting excited.

"You know the wonderful pastries they serve down at the Cove?"

"Yes. I've met Freddy. He's very talented."

"He's also very gone."

"What? Freddy? What happened to him?"

"I don't mean gone, that way. He's left town. He's joined the army. Well, he was already in the army, but just the reserves. Now he's signed up to serve full time. He just shipped out, and the Cove doesn't have a baker anymore. You haven't been down here the last few days. Poor Brenna's been serving store-bought pastries. She said the owners have been trying but can't find a baker to replace their son."

"You think they'd hire me?"

"Of course they would. I like your stuff every bit as much as Freddy's, if not more. But I wasn't thinking of them hiring you, not exactly."

"Then what are you—"

"I've got an idea. You don't have to do this. In fact, it's a pretty crazy idea. But if you and Dan like it, I think you could bake for the Cove *and* do your baking business, right here in their kitchen. And it wouldn't cost you a dime."

"Really? Are you serious? Oh, Diane, it sounds too good to be true. Really?"

"I think so. Do you have a minute for me to explain it?"

"Sure! Let me get the kids situated. It'll just take me a couple of minutes, and I'll call you right back."

"I'll be here." Diane hit End and stepped back into the Cove. "She's pretty excited about my idea, Brenna. It'll just be a few minutes. Are you sure you're okay waiting?"

"Take your time. I'll just finish cleaning up."

Diane went to sit at the nearest table by the door. Less than five minutes later, Shelley called her back. "I'll be right back, Brenna," she said and stepped outside again.

"Tell me everything, Diane."

"Okay, you already know about Freddy. Turns out, the Cove closes now at five, and it's going to stay that way at least until the spring. I was thinking, you could come here after they close and bake all the desserts they'd need for their pastry cabinet first. So they'd have plenty for the next morning. They'd pay for the supplies, so it wouldn't cost you anything, but you wouldn't charge them for filling up their cabinet.

"In exchange, they'd let you use their fully furnished, fully-permitted, commercial kitchen to bake anything you want for your baking business. Since you're planning to make it mostly an online business, after you bake what you need for business each day, you could bring it home and ship it from your house the next morning. I can't imagine there being any permits against that. And if you do have some local orders, people can pick them up from the Cove, maybe. So...what do you think?"

There was a long pause.

"Shelley, did I lose you?"

"Diane, I'm..."

Diane could hear her crying on the other end. "Hope those are tears of joy."

"Yes! They most certainly are. Diane, this is wonderful. It's more than wonderful!"

"So you like it?"

"I love it. It's perfect. This is the answer to our prayers. This is way better than Uncle Mike."

"Uncle who?"

"I'll explain later. I'm going to hang up. I want to call Dan right away."

"What are you going to tell him?"

"I don't know. Maybe to turn that truck around and come home. I'll call you later, and tell you what he says."

"So I can tell Brenna to call the owners of the Cove?"

"Tell her I'm definitely interested. Maybe you could get me the owners' phone number, and I'll call them after I talk to Dan."

"I'll do that."

"And, Diane . . . thank you *so* much. You are an incredible friend!"

"You're very welcome. You call Dan, and I'll explain everything to Brenna."

★   ★   ★

Shelley was actually trembling. Even with the two-key speed dial, she had to dial Dan's cell number twice.

"Hi, hon, is anything wrong? Is it one of the kids?"

"Everything's fine, the kids are fine," Shelley said. "Dan, the most incredible thing just happened. You're not going to believe it."

"What, in the last twenty minutes? I'm not even on the highway yet."

"Yes, I can't even believe it. I can't wait to tell you."

"So tell me."

"Okay. Dan, I think God has made a way for me to start the baking business, here in Marble Cove. We won't have to move, and it won't cost us a penny."

"What? Are you serious? How?"

"Isn't it wonderful?"

"I'm sure it is, but...how? How is that possible? Wait. I'm coming up to the highway exit."

"Can't you pull over?"

"Are you serious?"

"Dan, it's up to you, but I don't think you need to go to your Uncle Mike's tonight."

"You're that sure? Okay, I'm pulling over at a gas station. So tell me."

She explained Diane's idea, trying not to leave out a thing. When she finished, she said, "So, what do you think?"

"I'm stunned. The timing is just crazy."

"Isn't it? It's the light at the end of our tunnel." The verse Diane had told her about flashed through her mind.

"Are you sure you can do this bakery thing?" he asked. "It seems like a ton of work, especially after taking care of the kids all day. Baking all the Cove's stuff first, then yours, the same night, every night? Shipping it in the morning?"

"I know, it does. I don't have it all figured out. What I'd really like is for you and me to sit down and write everything out. But I did think about this one thing...I don't actually have any customers yet, and I wasn't even planning on launching the business until the fall fair. That's two weeks away. So, I'd have time to get used to baking things for the Cove way before I had to bake anything for my business."

"I wonder," he said. "I wonder if there'd be any harm if you baked the same things for both. When you did get started, I mean. Since all of your customers, most anyway, would be online, they'd be from out of town. It's not like there'd be a clash with local folks eating things you'd make at the Cove."

"That's a great idea. That way I'd be starting off just making bigger batches of the same things instead of lots of different desserts. I could get used to the kitchen and everything first. I have a feeling I can do this, Dan. What do you think? Do we say yes?"

There was a long pause. "I think so. But it's such a big deal. Maybe we should just say we're very interested and want to talk about the details some more. Like, when would they want you to start? Since they're not paying you, and your business won't start making any money for a while, I'll still need to keep my job at the dock. Who'd watch the kids?"

"I forgot to tell you. The Cove closes at five now. I wouldn't be coming in until after that. You're always home by then."

"Especially lately."

"So, I could watch the kids during the day. And then—"

"I'd be watching them while you're down there baking in the evenings?"

"Exactly. I know: it's not the best. You'd have to be a Mr. Mom a few hours every night."

"You think that's all it would be? A few hours a night?"

"I don't really know how long it'll take. I've never baked that much food before. Maybe for some parties or cookouts, but not in a commercial setup with all that nice equipment. I'm sure I'd get faster after I've done it awhile." She heard a sigh on the other end. "What's wrong?"

"Are you going to feel safe down there alone at night?"

Shelley wondered how much of this was just Dan feeling overwhelmed by the idea that he wouldn't be the main provider anymore if this idea worked. He'd opened up about this in that big talk they'd had earlier this month. "Dan, we've never felt afraid walking around Marble Cove at night. Nothing ever happens here, night or day. And I'll park the car in the street right by the front door."

"I guess."

"So what should I say? Should I call the owner?" She waited a moment.

"Shelley, I don't know how it will all come together, but my gut tells me this is what we've been praying for. It's an amazing opportunity."

"Really? Oh, Dan, thank you. I love you so much."

"I love you too."

"So I should call them?"

"Yeah. But, like I said, just to say we really want to talk about this with them in person. See when they can meet."

Her heart was pounding. It felt like her dream had risen from the dead. "What are you going to do now? You still going to go?"

"I'm going to call my Uncle Mike, tell him about this. Maybe he can buy some time with his painter friend until we get this sorted out."

"You're coming home?"

"I'm turning the truck around right now."

Shelley felt a girlish squeal threatening to burst out.

"You have any more of that blueberry crumb cake left?" he asked.

"Three slices."

"Then put on a pot of coffee, darlin', I'll be right home."

CHAPTER SEVENTEEN

Diane found herself worshipping at church Sunday morning with extra enthusiasm. It was so exciting how God had opened up this solution for Shelley's baking business—and for them to be able to stay in Marble Cove. She was so glad she'd gotten to play a part. It was almost like she'd been the matchmaker.

She had decided to take the entire day off from writing. She was now waiting for Shelley to call and fill her in. She and Dan were meeting with the owners of the Cove after church for lunch to talk everything out. Diane had already called Beverly and Margaret, without blowing the surprise, to tell them that something wonderful had happened and to see if they could come over to Diane's tonight around seven for dessert. She hoped to be able to tell them everything then. Both of them said they could come.

Diane was rinsing her lunch dishes in the sink when her cell phone rang. She looked over her shoulder and saw it sitting on the coffee table, the screen all lit up. Rocky stood beside it wagging his tail. "I'll get it, Rocky. Just gotta dry off my hands." She picked it up. The caller ID said it was Shelley calling. "Hello?"

"Diane, it's all set." She sounded so happy. "The lunch went wonderfully. I've never met those folks before, but they're very nice. And they're wide open to your idea."

"I'm so glad."

"They want to write everything we talked about in a contract. They're not going to hire a lawyer, since no money is changing hands. It's just to make sure everybody's on the same page about this, and everyone's in agreement about how it's going to work."

"Was Dan there?"

"Yes. In the car on the way home he said he felt even better about it now than last night."

"That's great!"

"They did ask for what I guess you'd call concessions from me, but I don't have a problem with them."

"Like what?"

"You know, Freddy had been making some things their customers love and ask for all the time. Like the poppy-seed muffins and—"

"The cheese Danishes?"

Shelley laughed. "And the cheese Danishes, and a few others. They were open to my making some of my specialties but wondered if I could keep making the things the regulars love."

"That should be easy for you."

"I'm up for it. They even have Freddy's recipes written down on index cards in a little box."

"And I'm sure in no time, some of your stuff will become things the regulars start ordering."

"I hope so."

"I know so."

"They also asked me if I could bake up some samples of the things I'd like to put in the cabinet for them, just to make sure they approve, before we start serving them to the public."

"Oh, Shelley, that's just going to make them more excited about having you there."

"You think?"

"They're going to love them, everything you make. We all do. I can't wait to see you tell Beverly and Margaret about this tonight."

"It's at seven, right?"

"Seven o'clock. Dessert and coffee."

"Sure. Dan said he'd watch the kids. They gave me Freddy's recipe box. I think I'm going to take a stab at his poppy-seed muffins this afternoon and bring them with me."

"Oh, Shelley." Diane released a contented sigh. "I'm so happy for you. I can't wait for tonight. Margaret and Beverly are going to be ecstatic too."

"It seems like we haven't all been together in forever."

"I know. See you at seven!"

★　★　★

Beverly and Margaret showed up right at seven. It took Shelley an extra fifteen minutes.

"Sorry I'm late," she said, as she walked through the door, carrying a tray. "Emma had a diaper incident. I didn't want to leave Dan with that."

"Oh my," Margaret said, already in her seat at Diane's table.

"Thought we'd meet in here instead of the living room," Diane said. "Are those the muffins?"

"They are."

"What kind?" Beverly asked.

"Poppy-seed," Shelley said.

"Like the ones down at the Cove?"

"Hopefully, Beverly, they are *exactly* like the ones down at the Cove." Shelley set the tray at the center of the dinette table and removed the aluminum foil.

"I'll take that," Diane said, pointing to the foil.

"Do you want to keep it to cover them after we're done?" Shelley asked.

"I don't think we're going to have any left," Diane said. "Tonight, we are celebrating."

"They look delicious," Margaret said.

"And," Diane added, peeking over Margaret's shoulder, "I'd say exactly like the muffins at the Cove. The coffee is ready. I'll pour it and bring the cream and sugar to the table."

"What's all this about?" Beverly asked. "Why are we celebrating, and why do we care if they look like the poppy-seed muffins at the Cove? Which they do."

"Shall I tell them or do you want to?" Shelley said to Diane.

"Shelley, you need to be the one to tell them. But let's wait one more minute. Everybody take a plate and a muffin. I'm pouring the last cup of coffee right…now." She carried the cups and set them down in front of each woman, then sat down with hers. "I'll say a quick blessing. Dear God, I thank You for this group of friends. Thank You for what You've done for Shelley and Dan. Thank You, especially that they don't have to move away from Marble Cove—"

"What?" both Beverly and Margaret said in unison.

Diane looked up at them impishly and added, "And I almost forgot. Thank You for these exquisite poppy-seed muffins. Amen."

Margaret looked at Shelley. "You don't have to move? What happened?"

"That's why we're celebrating," Diane said. "Okay, Shelley, tell them."

Over the next fifteen minutes, as they drank coffee and ate their muffins, Shelley told them the whole story, including the update from her lunch meeting with the Cove's owners. Everyone was so happy and excited.

"Did you talk to them about hoping to launch your business in time for the fall fair?" Beverly asked.

"Oh, I forgot to tell you. The answer is yes. They said if I wanted, I could use the sidewalk in front of the Cove for my baking business. They didn't see any conflict, since everything in their pastry cabinet would be on display anyway. That would draw plenty of visitors into the Cove. They said I can pass out brochures for my business right there and let everyone know they can get anything they see on display online. Of course, that's if we can get all of this figured out and set up between now and then."

"That's great," Diane said. "So you won't have to pay the fee for the vendor table."

"Isn't it?" Shelley said. "They've already sent the fee for the Cove in to city hall."

"So will everything you make for the Cove be the same as what you're selling yourself?" Beverly asked.

"I think so. At first, anyway," Shelley said. "Until I get a routine down. Then I can add new things to it as we go."

Margaret had a puzzled look on her face. "Did you ever get any replies from that want ad? For someone to do the brochures and Web sites?"

"We did get a handful of replies," Diane said, "but none of them panned out. They were mostly from high school kids. Their only samples were school projects they had done. I'm making progress on my proposals. I'm still holding out hope that I can do some work for you before the fair."

"I guess we haven't told you," Shelley said. "Beverly can do the Web sites and the brochures, and all in time for the fall fair." She looked at Beverly. "Oops. I guess I should have asked you first before saying that in front of everyone. Can you still do this?"

"Are you kidding? I can't wait to get started. My time isn't that crunched now anyway. I've asked Mrs. Peabody to stay on, helping at the house for at least another month or so."

Diane stood up. "I'm getting another cup of coffee. Anyone want some?"

"Oh dear," Margaret said. "In all this excitement, I forgot to ask if it was decaf. I'll be up all night."

"It's decaf," Diane said. "You're in the clear. Do you want some more? I made enough for everyone to have two."

Everyone asked for refills. After Diane poured them, everyone except Beverly went for a second poppy-seed muffin. Diane then set out a couple of pads of paper and some pens. "I thought while we're here, and the fall fair's just two weeks away, we can actually start hammering out what needs to be done."

"Great idea," Beverly said.

"But Diane," Margaret said, "are you sure you have time? Shouldn't you be working on your proposals?"

Diane smiled. "Tonight, I'm here for Shelley."

Shelley sniffled. "Thank you, Diane."

"Okay," Beverly said, grabbing the notepad and pen, "since I'm done eating, I'll go first. Shelley, didn't you say you were going to make samples of everything for the owners to taste?"

"Yes, starting with the muffins tonight. Then tomorrow I plan to start right in with everything else."

Beverly looked down at the lone muffin on the plate. "Do you have any more of these at home? I was thinking that we're going to need photos of everything for the Web site and brochures. I thought I might as well take pictures of them before you take them to the Cove."

"That's a great idea," Shelley said.

"But I'll need more than one of everything."

"I planned on baking a half-dozen."

"Perfect. I suppose you'll have to make some more of these muffins though."

"No, wait," Shelley said. "I left four of them at home for Dan. Let me call him right now and tell him hands off."

"He can eat one," Beverly said. "I'll add this one to it, and we'll just have four in that picture. Plus I can always duplicate one or more digitally to make it look like we've got more if I decide that's what the shot needs."

As Shelley called Dan to give him the bad news about the muffins, the ladies fixed their second cup of decaf. She got off the phone and said, "The poor thing. He had already eaten one and said he'd planned to polish off the others as soon as he put the kids down for bed. I told him that, after tomorrow, he'll have so many desserts around the house he might overdose on sugar."

They laughed. "That would be a problem for me," Margaret said. "Having all that dessert staring me in the face every day. I'd blow up like a balloon in a week."

"That's my self-control method," Beverly said. "I don't have it in the house."

"My self-control method," Shelley said, "is I don't feel like eating it after I've had my hands in it all day."

"Well, Shelley, I'll come over tomorrow afternoon with my camera and start taking pictures then." Beverly took a sip of coffee. "And we'll start talking about the kinds of words we want to use in the text areas. I'll look up some baking sites on the Internet to see what the norm is."

"I wish I could do the writing for you," Diane said. "I'm not quite at a place with my proposal where I can jump in."

"I'll tell you what you could do," Beverly said. "I'll write everything up the best I can over the next few days, and then you can be the editor. I'm more used to writing in a business style. But the text for this should be much prettier and fancier than that."

"I could probably swing that," Diane said.

"Hey, I just thought of something." Margaret's face lit up. "You should enter something in the annual bake-off contest at the fair, Shelley. You're a cinch to win it."

"That's a great idea," Diane said. "Think of all the extra publicity you'd get."

"I was thinking of doing that, back when I thought I could do the business out of my house. But then I gave the idea up when it seemed to fall through. Do you really think I can win?" Everyone agreed she could. "What should I make?"

"You don't have to decide now," Diane said. "Why don't you ask around, see what everyone says is their favorite? Like Dan's family—you've probably baked all your favorites for them over the years."

"That's a good idea," Shelley said. "They don't approve of everything I do, but they do always pick me to bring the desserts."

"And when you figure out what you're going to enter in the bake-off," Margaret said, "we can all come back here again for a taste test."

"Everyone who approves that idea, say aye," Diane said. "Good, the ayes have it."

CHAPTER EIGHTEEN

By midafternoon on Monday, Beverly had gotten all her work done for Phil Miller, her boss in Augusta. Even though Phil had been head of the department for only a short time, Beverly had been doing her job for so long that she could do some parts without expending any creative energy. Which left her mind free to think about this new, exciting project for Shelley. During her lunch break, she'd browsed the Internet looking at a number of online bakeries.

It was rather crazy, the more she thought about it. That something like this—an online bakery—even existed. She remembered how much fun she'd had as a girl going to the bakery with her mother. They were special memories. Were children today experiencing that? The only fresh-baked desserts available now in town were down at the Cove. And they had almost disappeared.

See what a heroic service you're supporting? she thought. But on the serious side, she really was doing more than just keeping the dream of fresh poppy-seed muffins and whoopee pies alive in Marble Cove. She was helping her friend Shelley Bauer make a go of a business that would keep her from having to move away. And that made her very happy.

Although her primary motive for moving to Marble Cove was to look after her father, her growing friendship with Shelley, Margaret, and Diane ran a close second. She hated the thought of this friendship changing radically, as would happen if Shelley were no longer a part. Beverly knew she'd always been on the shy side and was never one to make friends quickly. In fact, she wasn't sure she'd ever had more than one friend at a time, let alone been part of a foursome.

When she thought of the dynamics of this friendship, it didn't make a lot of sense. They were anything but a homogeneous fit, and really had almost nothing in common. But that didn't seem to matter. She'd really come to care about each of these women, and she was glad for the changes taking place in her heart.

An adventure, that's what her life was becoming, and she was so happy for it. She had been living for so long in what felt like a dark dream, shrouded in a gloomy haze. Good things were happening in her life, and she felt eager to see what might happen next.

She looked down at her watch, then closed the lid on her laptop. It was just about time to head over to Shelley's with her camera and for Mrs. Peabody to arrive to start dinner. She got up to check on her father. Before she'd even poked her head into the library, she heard his snoring. *Guess that answers my question about what you've been up to,* she thought.

His legs were propped up on his ottoman, and a book had slid down over his stomach. One arm dangled off to the side. The other was spread out across the end table. That concerned her a little. It was resting up against a coffee cup. She tiptoed over and carefully lifted the cup out of harm's way. As she stood up straight, a floorboard creaked.

"Huh? Oh, Beverly. It's you."

"Hi, Father. Catching a little nap?"

"I guess I was. Didn't plan to. I'm sleeping more than a cat these days."

She walked the cup toward the doorway. "Can I get you anything?"

"What time is it?"

"A little after three."

"Maybe a cold glass of water. My mouth's a little dry." He picked his book up and stared at it with a puzzled look.

"Don't know if you remember," Beverly said, "but I'll be heading over to Shelley's house across the street to take some pictures. You know the Bauers."

"Do I know the Bauers? Sure, I do. Not very well, I guess. Not exactly in my age bracket."

"Well, Mrs. Peabody should be here any minute. Then I'm going across the street."

"That's fine, dear. Don't worry about me. I'll be fine here."

She wished she could stop worrying about him. Even just a few months ago, she wouldn't have hesitated to leave him alone. She walked out to the kitchen, poured him a glass of ice water, and brought it to him. As she stepped back into the kitchen, the doorbell rang.

"Want me to get that, Beverly?" her father called.

"No, you stay put. It's probably just Mrs. Peabody." She walked to the door and opened it.

It was indeed Mrs. Peabody. "I'm sorry I'm a little late. Had to get a few things at the store for dinner."

If she was late, Beverly thought, it couldn't be more than a few minutes. "Not a problem, Mrs. Peabody." She stepped aside to let her in. "What are you making tonight?"

"I thought I'd make a meat loaf," she said, carrying in a few grocery bags.

"Can I help you with those?"

"They're not heavy." She walked them down the hall and into the kitchen. "I haven't made my meat loaf before, have I?"

"I don't think so."

"Well, I know you're probably thinking, Who likes meat loaf these days?"

Beverly wasn't thinking that at all. "I actually like—"

"But this isn't just any meat loaf. It's an old family recipe. Saw a recipe for one in a magazine the other day, and I've been craving it ever since. Especially since I know mine would put the one in that magazine to shame."

"What's in it?"

"For one thing, I don't just use hamburger. I mix in ground pork sausage. I also mix in a can of tomato sauce. And for a little kick, I toss in half a teaspoon of crushed red pepper."

"*Hmm*," Beverly said. "Sounds wonderful. But you might want to leave out the little kick. I'm worried about Father's stomach."

"I can do that. It doesn't change the taste that much. The mister will love it." She looked at Beverly, who was now holding her purse and camera. "Are you going somewhere?"

"I'm heading over to Shelley Bauer's house to take pictures."

"Of her children?"

"No, of a bunch of desserts she's making for the Cove. Did you know she was hoping to start a baking business?"

"I'd heard something about that, but I thought she was going to do it out of her house. That doesn't make a lot of sense to me. How do you run a bakery out of your house? People aren't going to want to come into someone's house to buy cakes and pies. Half the fun is walking into the bakery, looking at everything in the display case, smelling all those wonderful smells. I guess you'd still get all the nice smells in someone's house, but where would she put everything? On the coffee table? On the kitchen counter? I just couldn't see something like that working out very well."

Beverly smiled. It was an absurd scene to imagine. "Actually, she wasn't going to sell anything to customers in town out of her house. She'd be selling what she made over the Internet."

"Over the ... People do that?"

"Believe it or not. It's a thriving type of business now. Shelley can make something here, ship it to Vermont or wherever, and people there can serve it for dessert or at a party the next day."

"And it's still fresh?"

Beverly nodded.

"How is that possible?"

Beverly wasn't sure she understood all the details, or if Mrs. Peabody would understand the few things she did know. "All I know is that it definitely works. When I worked in Augusta, we'd ship baked goods as gifts to people all the time. And I got a few desserts in the mail myself. Last Christmas, someone sent me the most delicious cinnamon buns. I'd heat them up a little in the microwave, and you'd think they just came out of the corner bakery downtown."

"I guess if we can put a man on the moon...," Mrs. Peabody said.

"I guess," Beverly said. "It's amazing how the Internet has changed our lives."

"Hasn't changed mine any."

No, I suppose not, Beverly thought. Nor her father's, for that matter.

She realized how strange it must be for people in their generation to make sense of all this. Especially since she barely could herself. Just a few years ago, Beverly would have never thought about buying something over the Internet. Now she did it all the time. And here she was, helping her friend set up an online business...for shipping desserts, of all things.

"So you're going to be taking pictures of Shelley's baking business?" Mrs. Peabody asked.

"Yep. Of what she's cooking. Then we'll put them on a brochure and a Web site. It's kind of like an online version of the display case."

"But I thought I heard something happened, and she couldn't do it anymore."

Beverly glanced at her watch. She really needed to get over to Shelley's. "Well, that's all changed as of last night." She took a few minutes to tell Mrs. Peabody about the new development involving the Cove. When she got to the part about how they'd urged Shelley to enter this year's annual bake-off contest, she stopped short of mentioning much, especially the part about how certain they all were that she would win it.

Thankfully, Mrs. Peabody interrupted her at that moment. "Speaking of the bake-off, you know I won that several years in a row? With my chocolate cream pie. Another old family recipe."

"I remember your saying something about it." Beverly had also remembered her saying that she was much too old to do that sort of thing anymore.

"Well, I was going through some old boxes the other day, and I came across the one I kept all my blue ribbons in. Don't know what's come over me. Maybe it has something to do with getting out of the house every day to help out over here. Well anyway, it's kind of rejuvenated me, I guess. I've decided to enter my famous chocolate cream pie at the fall fair again this year. Lots of people have been asking me about it, saying they've missed seeing it at the bake-off these last few years. Have you ever tried it?"

Beverly thought a moment. "You know, I think I have. Not sure what year it was, but I was here visiting Father the weekend of the fair. And I do recall your winning that year."

"I made quite a few of them to serve to folks, not just the one I entered into the bake-off."

"I remember thinking it was delicious."

"Well, I'll tell you what...to help me sharpen up my skills, I'll make one this week for you and the mister. Let's see if I can make it as good as before."

"Well, you remember Father's a diabetic. He could eat only the smallest slice."

"Of course, dear," she said, as if talking to a child. "I'm not out to kill the man."

Beverly smiled. "I've really got to get across the street now. I'll be home before dinner."

"Okay then," she said.

Beverly headed toward the front door. Apparently, Shelley was going to have some stiff competition at the bake-off this year.

CHAPTER NINETEEN

As Beverly made her way across the street to Shelley's, she couldn't help but notice how the new autumn colors seemed more pronounced in the trees, both in the neighborhood and in the low hills to the west. It wasn't nearly as vibrant as it would be when it peaked, but it was noticeably brighter than even a week ago. She was no expert on fall foliage but it seemed to her that the leaves might actually peak very close to the fall fair, now less than two weeks away.

It'll be here before we know it, she thought. So much to do.

She looked to her right and saw Margaret's daughter Adelaide walking her way. A large tote bag hung over her shoulder, too big to be a purse.

"You going to visit Shelley now?" Adelaide yelled.

"I am, Adelaide. How are you doing this afternoon?"

"Fine," she said, a little quieter, now that she came closer. "I'm going to their house too. Shelley asked me to watch Aiden and Emma. I brought things to do with them." She pointed down to her bag. "Some coloring books and crayons. Some Lincoln Logs and Tinkertoys."

Beverly could hardly believe it. She had played with those as a child. "Are they very old?" They walked side by side now on the sidewalk.

"Some are." Adelaide stopped and opened the bag. "See, these ones are. But these ones"—she held up two sets of Tinkertoys that looked pretty much the same—"are only a year old. Mom says she thinks toys like these never grow old."

"I agree," Beverly said. Such fond memories.

"But," Adelaide said, a serious expression now, "we can't get these near baby Emma."

Beverly turned into Shelley's walkway. "That's true," she said. "We wouldn't want her to choke."

"She has to stay in the playpen when Aiden and I play." She stopped again. "I brought her picture books. See? With plastic pages, even if she puts them in her mouth, she can't hurt them."

Beverly looked but continued walking. She was already a few minutes late. Then she remembered that it didn't matter anymore. This wasn't the world of the State House of Representatives. She didn't have to worry about being "a few minutes late." Time moved much slower in Marble Cove than it did in Augusta. She sauntered up to the door and knocked gently in case one or both of the children were napping.

Beverly noticed the curtain in the living room open and close. "She's here!" a little boy yelled, obviously Aiden. "Adelaide's here." So much for being quiet. The front door opened. There stood Shelley, holding Emma sucking on a pacifier. Shelley smiled at Beverly. Emma's face lit up when she saw Adelaide. Beverly wondered how much they'd actually accomplish this afternoon and how many times the kids would draw Shelley away from their project.

"Hi, Emma," Adelaide said. "Hi, Aiden."

"You come to play with us?" Aiden asked.

"Yes," Adelaide said.

Both of them stepped inside. The house smelled wonderful. "I'm so excited you're here," Shelley said to Beverly. "I've been baking since before lunch." She moved to the side. "You can go on into the living room, Adelaide. Thanks so much for coming over."

"You're welcome. I love to help."

"Aiden, look at me." The little boy looked up into his mother's face. "You behave for Adelaide. Remember what I told you: Beverly and I have to work in the kitchen so we need you to stay in the living room."

"For how long?"

"Until she leaves."

"We won't be too long," Beverly said. "I'll be gone before you know it."

"Okay," he said and followed Adelaide into the living room.

"Adelaide," Shelley said, "aren't you forgetting someone?"

Adelaide turned. "Oh, Emma." She walked back. Emma reached out for her, a big smile appearing behind her pacifier. She picked her up and carried her into the living room.

"They'll be fine," Shelley said. "They love Adelaide."

"I can see that."

"Well"—Shelley turned toward the kitchen—"are you ready to take some pictures?"

"Let's do it."

They walked toward the wonderful smells. Beverly had been to Shelley's house a number of times, but she hardly recognized the kitchen. Every spare inch of the counter was covered by something: bags of flour, bags of sugar (brown and white), cartons of eggs, mixing bowls of various sizes, cookie sheets, bowls of blueberries, chopped apples, chunks of pineapple, and a box of granola cereal.

"I know," Shelley said. "It looks crazy in here. But there's a method to my madness."

"As long as it makes sense to you," Beverly said. "It's how it tastes, right, not how it looks getting made?"

"I'm glad it's not a cooking show," Shelley said. "And you only have to take pictures of the dessert dishes, right? Not of me. Please say yes."

"This afternoon, that's right. But sometime I need to take some pictures of you. In the next day or two, preferably."

"I'll worry about that when the time comes." Shelley wiped her forehead with a dish towel. "Are you sure we can't hire a model and say she's me?"

Beverly smiled. "Relax, Shelley. I've seen you cleaned up. You'll be perfect."

"I guess," she said. "I can't wait to start baking over at the Cove."

"Have you seen the kitchen there?"

"Yes. Compared to this, it will be incredible. So much more room to work."

"And I'm guessing you can bake a lot more in less time."

"That too," Shelley said. "Over here, we have the end result." She pointed toward the table. It was covered as well, but with dishes and platters filled with finished desserts. "On the corner of the hutch there, I've got a small stack of magazines. I put Post-its on pages with pictures of dessert dishes. Thought it might give you some ideas."

"That's great, Shelley. I've also been checking lots of food Web sites for the same reason. In my bag here, I've brought some little props that might help make things prettier."

"I've got some silk flowers and this cornucopia thing here," Shelley said. "The fruit is fake, but it looks pretty real. We'll have to see how it looks on camera, then decide. As you can see, it's all in fall colors."

"I think that's a good idea. We should go with a fall theme. It will only be good for a couple of months, but that's the beauty of doing the Web site yourself. You can change everything pretty easily. After Thanksgiving, or maybe just before, we can take some new pictures with a Christmas theme. Then just switch them out. After Christmas, we'll take the Christmas pics out but keep a wintry theme going until the spring."

"You've really thought this thing out. I don't know the first thing about Web sites."

"Well...I don't bake. Besides, this software I'm using is pretty easy to work with."

"But what about the brochures?" Shelley said. "I'm guessing they won't be so easy to change."

"You'd be surprised. Not too many years ago, it would have been a nightmare. Just to get a decent price, they used to make you print a minimum of five hundred or a thousand. It would get ridiculously expensive making new brochures for every season. But now, it's not hard at all. Everything's digital: the pictures, the printers. We can pretty much print out however many we think we need. If we run out, we'll just print some more. Really, it won't be that much harder than changing the Web site."

"Beverly, I'm so glad you're doing this."

"Well...I hope you feel that way when I'm done. Like I said, I'm not a pro. And honestly, if your business takes off, and you want to hire someone to do the Christmas shots or redo anything I've done, I won't be offended."

"I'm sure it will be great," Shelley said. "So where do you want to start?"

Beverly looked down at all the dessert dishes spread out on the table. She immediately recognized those scrumptious poppy-seed muffins and cheese Danishes. Then a whole assortment of whoopie pies in numerous colors and sizes. One group was even shaped into little clams. In the corner several different "dirt" recipes were on display: dirt cake, dirt pie. "Oh my," she said, pointing at those.

"I know," Shelley said. "But the kids love it."

Beverly didn't know what lay underneath, but the tray was covered with crumbled Oreos, looking very much like rich topsoil. Lying here and there on top of the "dirt" were gummy worms. "I'm sure they do." Beverly pointed at a delicious-looking blueberry crumb cake. "Now, that's how you can pay me."

"It is *so* good," Shelley said. "Don't even ask me how much butter I put in that thing. I've actually made two. Dan loves it. When we're done, we'll each have a slice over coffee, and you can take the whole one home."

"Oh, we won't need a whole one. It's just me and Father, and I have to keep him away from too many sweets to keep his blood sugar managed. Mrs. Peabody would probably take some too."

"Seriously," Shelley said. "You're going to have to help me get rid of some of this. The kids will be like wild animals for days if I let them eat all this sugar. And we can't afford to put Dan in a new pants size."

"I'll take some of it," Beverly said. "Maybe we should call Margaret and Diane after we're done and let them dive in."

"Good idea. How much time will this take? Should I start the coffee?"

"Not just yet," Beverly said. "Let me look at this for a minute. As a photographer, not as a customer." She looked around at the lighting in the dining area. "I'm glad it's a sunny day. We'll need all the light we can get. The colors in the pictures come out much nicer when there's plenty of light. Why don't we do this—let's take everything off this end of the table. We'll make it our little display area. I love the tablecloth."

Over the next forty-five minutes, Beverly and Shelley worked together, experimenting with design ideas, photographing each dessert in a variety of ways, playing with the light, and using all the little props. Before changing to a new dish, Beverly would pull the little storage card out of her camera so they could see the pictures enlarged on her laptop. When they were done, Beverly had plenty of photographs to play with back at her place.

Beverly began photographing the last dessert, the dirt cake with the gummy worms. "Now you can put the coffee on." As she snapped away, she could easily see kids loving a dessert like this but, for her, it was close to revolting. "Shelley, have you decided which of these desserts you're going to enter into the bake-off? Please don't say it's this one."

Shelley laughed. "No. I'm not even sure I'll bring the Gummy Worm Dirt Cake down to the Cove. That one's strictly for a kid section I'd like to make for the Web site." She brought out the sugar and creamer and set it on the table. "I'm not sure yet which one to use for the bake-off. I'm pretty sure it's not going to be any of these."

"Well, whichever one you pick, it would probably be good to get some pics of it for the Web site. Because it will probably win, and then we can make a big fuss of that on the home page. Speaking of the bake-off, looks like you might be having some stiff competition this year."

"Really?"

"Mrs. Peabody's going to enter the contest this year."

"She is? I thought she had stopped doing that."

"She did. But just before I left the house, she told me she might jump in again this year. Whatever you make, it will be going up against Mrs. Peabody's award-winning chocolate cream pie."

Shelley frowned.

"What's the matter?" Beverly asked.

"Have you tasted Mrs. Peabody's chocolate cream pie?"

"It's pretty good," Beverly said.

"Pretty good?" said Shelley. "It's more than pretty good. I don't think I have a chance of winning now."

CHAPTER TWENTY

The following week seemed to zip right by, and now it was Friday evening. The previous night, Shelley had passed the Cove's owners' taste test with flying colors. They had eaten her samples at the store by themselves, after closing for the day. Shelley had been so nervous waiting for their call.

But they had loved what she baked, every single thing. They'd asked her and Dan to come by so they could show her where everything was and how the kitchen equipment worked.

This evening, she was on her own. The Cove's kitchen was hers to command.

"I am so nervous," she said to Dan.

He was helping her unload supplies from the car. They had pulled his pickup truck to the Cove's back door. After this, he planned to head home and relieve Diane, who was watching the kids.

"Shelley," he said, "you're going to do fine. They loved everything. Just make everything the same way you do it at home." He walked through the door and held it open with his foot, so she could come in. "The only difference is, you're making a lot more of everything."

She walked past him and through the hallway, carrying a box with cartons of cream cheese. "But what if I get the measurements wrong? People are going to be coming here tomorrow morning expecting a pastry cabinet full of desserts."

The back door slammed as he came in behind her, carrying big bags of flour. "And that's exactly what they're going to see," he said. "We went over the math a dozen times. It all worked out. Do you have the schedule we put together?" He set the flour on a large work table.

"It's right here. At least I think it is." She quickly rummaged through her purse. "Here it is."

Dan walked over and stood close. "Then all you have to do is follow what you've written down," he said calmly. "It's a solid plan. You've thought it all through. You're going to be fine." He took hold of her shoulders and turned her around to face the kitchen. "Shelley, look at this. Look at that huge baking oven. Look at those shelves and that pantry filled with everything you need to bake with. Look at that huge double-door fridge, that stainless steel sink and commercial dishwasher." He turned her head to the right. "Look at that butcher-block work table. There's three times the workspace there than in our entire kitchen."

"I know." She couldn't restrain her smile.

"A week ago, I was driving to my Uncle Mike's, hoping to get a painting job in Portland."

"I know."

"And we thought we might have to have to leave Marble Cove."

"I know. Look at what God has done." She reached up and hugged him. Her fears had melted away completely.

"I'll make one last trip out to the truck," he said, "just to make sure we didn't forget anything. Now are you sure you feel absolutely safe in here by yourself?"

"I do. You'll double-check all the doors and lock me in. Then I'll call you when I'm almost done."

He headed down the hallway. She turned back around, faced her new kitchen, and took a deep breath. "Time to get to work."

★   ★   ★

The next morning, Diane walked into the library and sat at the "lookout table" by the front window. It was time for her shift. Margaret was staring out the front window and didn't notice her. As soon as Diane saw the bored look on Margaret's face, she knew nothing had happened on her watch.

The past week, Diane had kept tabs on everyone mostly by phone, since she had been working furiously on her three-book proposal.

Beverly had continued putting Shelley's Web site and brochure together in her off-hours. She said she was starting to get the hang of doing her day job at home now. Her boss seemed happy with things. She'd told Diane that she was definitely glad she'd kept Mrs. Peabody on. She didn't see how she could have created the Web site for Shelley if she'd also had to do all the work Mrs. Peabody had taken off her hands.

Diane had called Beverly last night to see if either she or Shelley had spotted their mysterious stranger Thursday afternoon during their stakeout at the library. Neither one had. Beverly had hinted at the idea of dropping the stakeout. Diane hadn't said anything then, but standing there now, looking at Margaret, she wished she had. She was scheduled to sit there for two more hours, relieving Margaret so she could open up her gallery on time.

But Diane also had plans to stop by the Cove this morning. When she'd called Shelley last night, she'd learned that all the baked goods in the pastry cabinet this morning had been made by Shelley last night.

"Hi, Margaret," Diane said, setting her laptop case on the table.

Margaret looked up, startled. Then she laughed. "You scared me again. Guess it doesn't take much."

"No sign of our mysterious stranger?"

"Nope. Just the usual Saturday morning suspects walking the streets of Marble Cove, doing what they always do on a Saturday morning. From what I hear, no one saw him on Thursday either."

"No, they didn't," Diane said.

"I'm thinking this might turn out to be a fool's errand." Margaret stood and gathered her things. "I think our young man may have found all he was looking for already, and he's not coming back."

"I'm inclined to agree. I think I'm going to call Beverly after I put in my time here and suggest we let this thing go."

"When you call her, tell her that's my vote too."

"I will. How are things coming along with your paintings?"

"Wonderful. I think I'll finish up my second one for Lighting the Way this afternoon, depending on how things go at the gallery. I sold two more paintings this week, so that's helped our cash flow. Of course, it made the gallery look even more empty."

"Did you happen to take pictures of them, so you can make prints of them later on?"

"I did. Actually, I took pictures of all of them. But I was doing that before. We'll be ready to start making those giclée prints of everything as soon as we get some time on our hands. Of course, my little camera can't produce high enough resolution photos. The print house will take care of that."

Margaret raised her index finger. "I have something else to tell you. I've been talking about the print idea with everyone who's shown interest in one of the paintings at the gallery. The ones who usually just leave empty-handed. You were right: they were all happy to hear about it, and every single one put their name down on that clipboard. They left their e-mail addresses so I can contact them whenever we get it going."

"See? I knew that would happen. Your gallery is going to take off once you get that up and running."

"Well, I better get over there and open up. Let me know if you see our tall, dark stranger." She smiled conspiratorially.

"I will."

Diane spent the next ninety minutes reading and typing notes, looking up every time someone walked into the library, then down the street at the front door of the *Courier*. She didn't see a single person she could classify as mysterious or strange. Her cell phone started to vibrate on the table. She picked it up and looked at the screen. It was Beverly.

"Hey, Diane."

"Hi, Beverly."

"No luck?"

"Nope."

"I'm sorry. It was a lame idea."

"No, it wasn't. We wouldn't have thought that if one of us had spotted him."

"I suppose," Beverly said. "But look, I'm sure you've got better things to do than sit there at the library."

"Nonsense. I've got my laptop. I can work anywhere. Besides, I've only got another thirty minutes on my shift."

"That's okay. Really. You don't need to sit there any longer. I think we should officially call off our stakeout."

Diane laughed. It really did sound silly to call it that.

"How are things coming with your book proposal, by the way?"

"Very well...I think. I won't know, of course, until I turn it in. My agent might hate it."

"I doubt that. Are you getting close to sending it in?"

"Maybe. I might finish it today. I won't send it in though. She asked me to get it to her by the end of the month, so I still have another week to sit on it. I'll probably rewrite it a dozen times between now and then. What are your plans for today?"

"I'm probably at the same stage with Shelley's Web site and the brochure. Feels like I'm almost done, but I want it to be perfect. So I'll keep tweaking it. Not ready to launch it until we get a little closer to the fall fair. Did you get to try any of the desserts you took home a few days ago?"

"Are you kidding? They're all gone, and they were delicious. My blood sugar hasn't dipped in days. I'm heading over to the Cove right now."

"That's right," Beverly said. "Today's the big day, isn't it?"

"Yep. Everything in the pastry cabinet today should have been made by Shelley last night."

"I wonder how it went."

"I'll let you know."

★　　★　　★

When Diane walked into the Cove, it wasn't packed, but it was far more crowded than she'd seen it since Labor Day. Half the tables were filled, and three customers stood in front of her at the counter. She stepped over and glanced at the pastry cabinet, instantly recognizing Shelley's handiwork. Every tray had something on it, but most were half-empty, and it wasn't even noon yet. She got back in line and waited her turn.

"How ya doing, Diane?" Brenna said, as she stepped to the counter. "You want your usual latte?"

"I do, but the cupboard looks a little bare over there. I was in the mood for one of those poppy-seed muffins today."

"Sorry, all gone."

"So I guess there's none in the back."

"Nope, sorry. Not sure today's a good day to judge quantities, seeing as it's a Saturday. But I've been here a lot of Saturdays. Don't recall the cabinet being so empty this early in the day. Not since the height of summer. Guess we'll have to wait and see what happens during the week, but I'm thinking we might have to get Shelley to make quite a few more of everything."

"Didn't she make enough?"

"Oh no, she made all we asked for. I'm just saying, folks can't get enough." She leaned over the counter to speak quietly. "If I were you, I'd get a slice of that blueberry crumb cake, right they-ah on the second row. It's incredible. Some folks have come back for a second slice of that one. The few that are left will be gone within the hour." Brenna handed her the latte.

"Then I'll have that." Diane had actually eaten it before, about a month ago when she'd visited Shelley's house. Brenna put it on a plate for her with a fork. Diane paid her and turned to look for a seat. It was pretty crowded in here. If she wanted to get any work done on her proposal she'd need to use her earbuds to pipe in some music. She sat at a nearby empty table, set her bag in the seat beside her and took a bite of the crumb cake.

Oh my, she thought. It was even better than she remembered. She took a few more bites and sipped her latte. Motion caught her eye, and she looked up at the front door.

August Jackson walked in, his face all smiles. "Say, Brenna. Guess I better get in here and see what all the fuss is about."

"You mean about our new baker?"

"That's what I'm hearing. I must have bumped into three or four people this morning all saying I should come right over here and get one of these treats before they're all gone."

"Then I guess you better pick something out while I get your mug of java."

He turned and saw Diane, then stepped over to her table. "So, did you ever meet up with that man asking about the lighthouse?"

"I'm afraid not, Augie. It wasn't for a lack of trying."

"No? Too bad. Did you catch him this morning?"

"No."

"He's here in town, saw him myself not twenty minutes ago."

Diane sat straight up. "Really? Where?"

"Coming out of the *Courier*."

"That's impossible. I was right there at the library watching for him."

Augie got a confused look on his face. "I don't know what to say. I'm sure it was him."

"Did you talk with him?"

"No, he was too far away. Suppose I could have chased him. Now wouldn't that have been a sight?"

Diane stood up. "Do you know which way he went?"

"Which way?" He thought a moment. "I suppose he went up the street, the opposite direction from the library. Guess that's why you missed him."

Diane felt silly. She was tempted to run right out after him. "Twenty minutes ago?"

He nodded. "Maybe thirty."

"Here's your coffee, Augie," Brenna yelled from the counter.

"Thanks, Brenna." He turned back to Diane. "If I see him again, I'll tackle him and hold him down until you get there."

She smiled. "Now that's a sight I'd like to see."

*   *   *

The sun had started to set. Mrs. Peabody had said dinner would be ready in thirty minutes. Beverly had been in the house all day, and she just had to get out and get some fresh air. She wanted to go for a run, but she knew she'd get all sweaty and not have enough time to take a shower when she got home.

A brisk walk down the boardwalk walkway, then. The air didn't get any fresher than it was down by the beach. She put on her sweats and sneakers and headed out the door. She didn't see any of her friends as she walked by their houses. Rocky barked a hearty hello as she passed Diane's bungalow.

Within fifteen minutes she was down at the far end of the boardwalk. She needed to turn around now if she wanted to get back in time for dinner. As she turned, she now faced the lighthouse. She looked at it out of habit, then stopped in midstep.

She couldn't believe it: a light was shining near the top. Not the big light that shone out over the water, but the kind of light they had all seen before, as if someone was walking around inside carrying a lantern. Instantly, she remembered her phone call with Diane this afternoon saying that August Jackson had seen their mysterious stranger in town.

It had to be him.

Heading back, she picked up her pace and soon reached the spot on the boardwalk closest to the beach. It was the moment of decision. If she stayed on the boardwalk, she'd make it home in time for dinner. But if she took off running down the beach, she might just catch whoever was inside.

She wasn't a little girl anymore. It wasn't as if she'd get a talking-to for coming home late.

She took off running down the beach, her eyes constantly on the lighthouse. She had maybe five minutes left to close the gap when the light suddenly went out. *Oh no,* she thought. Now she ran as fast as she could. It was darker on the beach, but she didn't worry, because it was low tide.

She should have.

A moment later, she tripped over a piece of driftwood and went flying. She landed facedown in the hard sand. She felt the air forced out of her lungs as she made contact.

She lay there a moment trying to sort out what just happened. Slowly, she began taking inventory, moving first her feet, then her legs, then her hands and arms. Nothing seemed broken or even sprained. A few seconds later, her breathing returned to something like normal.

She sat up and moved her neck back and forth. It seemed okay. As she rose to her feet, however, she felt a spasm of pain in her back. She must have twisted it as she fell. She began some stretch routines, trying to relieve the pain.

The lighthouse was still dark. She could start running again and maybe...*maybe* get there before the mysterious stranger had left. But she doubted it. Plus, she wouldn't be running so much as hobbling. And she felt silly even thinking about trying.

She was an adult, after all. This wasn't some Nancy Drew mystery.

It was time for dinner.

She turned around, brushed the sand off, and headed toward the promenade.

Chapter Twenty One

Margaret had a wonderful time at church this morning. She loved those weeks when things went well enough that you didn't feel you needed to make it to church just to survive the week to come. She'd had plenty of Sundays like that. Quite a few over this past summer. But things were going well these days, and she was grateful for the respite from trouble and woe.

She'd finished her second painting for the greeting card company yesterday. This was the one that showed the lighthouse in spring, and it had turned out as nicely as she had hoped. Allan was happy with his new furniture orders and hoping to get more from the fall fair next week. Yesterday afternoon, he'd brought a number of new pieces down to the gallery that he'd finished on Friday.

One good thing about that: all this furniture gave the gallery a full feeling. Initially, the idea was just to have a few pieces placed strategically here and there, as accents. But now Allan actually had more pieces of furniture in the gallery than Margaret had paintings left to sell. She'd joked with him, after he set the last piece down yesterday, that maybe they should change the name of the place to "Allan's Furniture Emporium."

Adelaide had had a nice week too. Sadly, Dan's work was still very slow. He got off most days at lunch, so he was able to watch the kids in the afternoon. But Shelley had been so busy baking all week that she'd asked Adelaide if she could come over and watch her kids three or four mornings in a row. It was good for Adelaide to stay busy, and she really enjoyed spending time with Aiden and Emma.

At the moment, her soul full from church and her stomach full from lunch down at Captain Calhoun's Crab and Lobster House, Margaret was ready for a nap. She was about to check in with Allan and Adelaide to see if they needed anything when her cell phone rang. She hurried around the living area, trying to find the stupid thing before it went to voice mail.

There it was on the edge of the coffee table, under a magazine, of all places. She lifted it up and read the screen. No name. Whoever it was, he or she wasn't on her list of contacts. She sighed, wondering if she should bother. Before she'd given it another thought, it stopped ringing. A few moments later, she got the little beep that meant someone had just left her a message.

That's fine, she thought. She'd leave it alone and listen to it after her nap.

She set it back on the coffee table—in plain sight, this time—and turned to walk away. A few steps farther, she stopped, realizing that she'd never be able to nap in peace without knowing who it was or why they had called. She walked back, picked it up, and dialed her voice mail number. Her face lit up when she heard the message:

"Hi, Margaret. I'm not sure we've met. My name is Madeleine Bancroft. I'm in charge of the fall fair this year, and I have some exciting news to share with you. Could you call me as soon as you get this message?"

Margaret called her back immediately. "Hi, Madeleine. This is Margaret Hoskins returning your call."

"Hi, Margaret, thanks for calling me back so fast. Is your gallery open this afternoon, by any chance?"

"My gallery? Why, no. I wasn't planning on opening for another hour or so."

"I see. I'd like to meet you there later on, if I could. I've got a lot of errands to take care of downtown. You know the fall fair starts Friday, and I have a ton of things left to do."

"Congratulations. I heard the town council picked you to run things this year."

"Thanks. As it turns out, congratulations are in order for you, as well. That same town council has picked you to do something this year. It was actually my idea, but they jumped at it as soon as I brought it up."

"Really? What is it?"

"I'd rather tell you about it in person. If you agree, we have a number of things to work out, and I'd like to check this off my list. Today, if possible. How about in an hour, when you open up?"

"I can do that," Margaret said. They exchanged good-byes and Margaret disconnected.

She wondered what on earth it could be.

⋆　　⋆　　⋆

Margaret sat on a chair at the cash register inside the gallery. She'd turned the sign to read Open, but so far no one else had come in. Madeleine Bancroft had just called saying she was sorry she was late but was just around the corner.

Margaret had thought about turning on the coffeepot to make just enough for two cups, but it seemed Madeleine was in quite a hurry.

As she sat there, she reflected on what Beverly had told her about seeing a light from the lighthouse. Apparently Beverly had been running down the beach and had fallen and hurt herself. Not too bad, it seemed, but still—what had she been thinking? It was odd what each of them had done in the pursuit of this lighthouse mystery.

Margaret looked up, and there was Madeleine walking through the front door.

"Come in, Madeleine."

"Thanks so much for seeing me. I'm running around these days like a crazy person. Every time I check something off my list, three new things seem to appear out of nowhere." She shook Margaret's hand. "Please call me Maddie."

"Okay, Maddie. Come on in and have a seat, right next to me." She flicked on a little lamp sitting on one of Allan's end tables. "So what's this all about?" Margaret spotted a manila folder wedged under Maddie's arm.

Maddie pulled it out and opened it on the desk. "I guess you could say it's about this." Margaret looked down and saw a copy of the *Courier*, the one with her picture on the front page. "I knew you had started this gallery, but I had no idea you were such an accomplished artist." Maddie looked around at the paintings on the wall. "Is the one from the newspaper still here?"

"No, I had to ship that to the greeting card company." She turned around and pointed to the easel. "But I just finished the second one for them yesterday. I'll be shipping that out on Monday."

"You must be thrilled to have so many more people getting a chance to admire your work." Maddie stood up and walked to the easel. Margaret flipped on a little light just above it. "My, it's beautiful," Maddie said.

"I'm glad you like it."

"When will they start showing up on cards?"

"I don't know exactly. I think it says something about that in my contract, but I don't remember right now."

They walked back and sat by the checkout counter. "Well, I better get right to the point," Maddie said. "Did you know we're going to be starting an art contest at the fall fair? I'm hoping to make it an annual thing."

"I think I read something about it on a flyer," Margaret said.

"It's called the Chalk Walk Contest. We're going to block off the whole sidewalk area in front of the library and divide it into three age groups. Elementary, middle school, and high school. And we're going to invite young artists from our local schools to each take a little square and draw whatever they want using chalk we'll provide. It washes off pretty easily."

"Are you sure you have enough squares on the sidewalk?" Margaret said. "Seems like a lot of kids might want to do something like that."

"Good point. The school teachers did their own minicontests in classrooms this week to whittle the numbers down. I haven't gotten the names of the finalists yet, but they're supposed to choose six children from each age group, for a total of eighteen squares."

"That's a good idea."

"Well, here's the best part...the town council members and I want you to serve as our judge. We want you to pick the winners of the contest. One from each age group. And then a grand prize winner out of the three."

"You want *me* to be your judge?"

"Yes! Oh, Margaret, you'd be perfect. And the kids would be so honored. Everyone in town knows about your work now. I hope you don't mind, but I told the art teachers we would be asking you. But they didn't tell the kids because we hadn't asked you yet. They just said we had a renowned artist coming to serve as our judge."

A renowned artist? Margaret thought. That seemed a bit overstated. Nevertheless, she was honored, if not overwhelmed. "Well, I...I think I'd be delighted to serve as your judge."

"Thank you! I so hoped you'd say yes."

"Well, thank you, Maddie. I think I'll enjoy this. I love working with kids."

"There's one other detail I want to mention. There's no money available to pay for y—"

"Don't even think about it," Margaret said. "I wouldn't take any money if you offered it. It will be my pleasure."

"Thanks," Maddie said. "But I did ask the council to approve one budget item for this: a grand prize for the overall winner." She got up and walked to one of the smaller paintings hanging on the wall. "I'm going to see if they'll approve enough money to buy one of your paintings, maybe a smaller one like this, and give it to the winner. I just think that would mean so much more than a blue ribbon. We'll set it up on an easel right in front of the library all day Sunday, marking it as the grand prize."

Margaret didn't know what to say. But she got an idea. "I'll tell you what, Maddie, you and the council use that money for something else. I'd like to donate this painting to the fall fair and present it to the winner myself."

Maddie's eyes got big and wide. "You'd do that? Why, Margaret, we couldn't ask you to—"

"You didn't ask. It's my treat."

"That's wonderful, Margaret. Thank you so much. I'll make sure we get you a letter from the city, acknowledging your donation."

"My husband's a retired CPA," Margaret said. "I'm sure he'll appreciate that." And Margaret was a retired bookkeeper. She knew deductions like this came in handy at tax time.

"I'm so glad I thought of you for this," Maddie said. "And so glad we could take care of all of this today. I'll get the word out to everyone right away."

"I'll look forward to it," Margaret said.

Maddie closed her manila folder and headed to the front of the gallery. "I'll probably be calling you sometime midweek just to firm up any last-minute details." She stuck out her hand and Margaret shook it again. "I hope the rest of the things on my checklist go as well as this," she said and headed out the door.

Margaret walked to the window and pressed her forehead against the glass. "Thank You, Lord," she said aloud, "for blessing me like this."

CHAPTER TWENTY-TWO

Later that afternoon, after she'd closed the gallery for the day, Margaret filled Allan in on all the exciting news about the town council picking her to be the judge for the new Chalk Walk Contest. He had been out in his workshop, tidying up a bit.

He set his broom aside. "I'm proud of you," he said. "Now the whole town's going to know how talented you are." It was sweet. "So let's not hear any more jokes about Allan's Furniture Emporium. Have you picked out which painting you're going to give to the winner?"

She had, and she told him which one. "I've already taken it down and set it behind the counter. Of course, it was the only painting left on that section of the wall."

"This thing is really bugging you, isn't it?" he said. "I don't mind taking out some of my furniture pieces, if you think it'll help...at least until after the fall fair."

"That's only going to make it worse," she said. "The gallery will really look empty then." She sighed. "I just wish there was a way for me to start that giclée printing thing now. Those samples I ordered look amazing. But I did a little more research while I was doing my rotation at the library the other day. It seems we need not only someone to do the printing but also someone to stretch the canvases over a frame. Most of these printers offer that service, but the difference in price between just the canvas print rolled up and sent to me and having it sent to me on a wood frame is huge. Wish we could do that part ourselves. Oh, there's so much to think about."

"Well, don't worry about it. These really are good problems. Do you remember back in July? You thought you'd have to close it down altogether, right? We'll get this thing sorted out."

"I know," she said. "Guess I'll head into the house. I'm going to fix some coffee. Want some?"

"A cup of coffee would be great about now."

As she walked out of the garage onto the driveway, Margaret noticed Shelley pushing a stroller across the street. Little Aiden walked beside her. Shelley didn't look very happy. She had the same fretful look on her face that she often wore these past few months, ever since the cutbacks had started with Dan's job. Lately though, Shelley had seemed almost radiant by comparison, now that her new baking business was back on track. So it was strange that she would be low again now.

Margaret waved to her. Shelley glanced her way, offered a quick smile and an even quicker wave back, and kept walking. Something was definitely troubling her. Margaret walked toward the sidewalk. "Hey, Shelley."

Shelley stopped and turned around. "Hi, Margaret. Thought I'd just take the kids out for some fresh air. I've been so busy lately that I've hardly had a moment to enjoy this beautiful weather. And it won't stay like this for long."

"It really is so nice out. I love September. Not just because of the cooler temperature. Even more because of all the colors in the trees." Margaret walked across the street toward her. "Is everything all right?"

"I'm...okay. I'm just trying to get used to this new schedule, I think."

"Is everything going okay down at the Cove?"

Shelley's face brightened. "It's been great. I can't believe the reaction I'm getting from the customers. The owners told me they've had better sales out of the pastry cabinet this week than during their busiest week this summer."

"How wonderful," Margaret said. "I'm not at all surprised."

"Mommy, are we still going for a walk?"

Shelley looked down at Aiden. "We are, but shouldn't you be saying hi to someone?"

Aiden looked up, squinting his eyes in the sun. "Hi, Miss Margaret. We're going for a walk now."

That last line sounded like Aiden's way of saying *You can leave now*. Margaret laughed. "And hello to you, Aiden."

"I'm sorry," Shelley said. "I've been promising to take them for a walk all weekend."

"And I'm slowing you down. I just haven't seen you all week. I wanted to say hi and see how you're doing."

"Actually," Shelley said, almost in a whisper, "I'm struggling a little about something. Would love to talk to you about it sometime."

"I thought so."

"Is it that obvious? All the way across the street?"

"It's just that you've been so happy lately." Margaret looked down at Aiden. He was gently pulling on Shelley's pant leg.

"I am happy," she said. "Mostly. But look, duty calls."

"If you want, I could ask Adelaide to watch them. I think she's free. I was just about to put some coffee on for Allan and me."

Shelley looked down at Aiden. "How would you like it if Adelaide watched you and Emma for a little while?"

"No! I want the park! You promised!"

"You're right, I did." Shelley turned to Margaret. "Do you think we could all walk to the park and Adelaide could watch them there while we talk?"

"Yay!" Aiden said.

"I'll go ask her and make sure," Margaret said. "You wait right here." She hurried across the street and found Adelaide reading a book in her room. "Adelaide, I want to talk with Shelley for a little while at the park. Would you be willing to come so you could watch Aiden and Emma?"

Adelaide looked up. "Sure. When?"

"Right now. They're right outside."

"Really?" She got up and walked past her and out the front door. Not a moment's hesitation. Adelaide was always so eager to serve others. By the time Margaret got to the doorway, Adelaide was already across the street greeting the children. Aiden actually jumped up and down.

"Thank you so much, Adelaide," Shelley said.

They walked the rest of the way to the park, chatting amiably. When they reached the playground, Aiden ran to the play equipment, and Adelaide carried Emma to the baby swings. Margaret and Shelley sat at a picnic table in the shade where Shelley could keep an eye on the playground.

"Well, start talking," Margaret said.

Shelley reached toward Margaret's face. "You've got a little . . . crumb or something."

Margaret wiped at it and looked at her fingers. "Oh, you caught me. It's from this incredible blueberry crumb cake a friend of mine makes. You should have some. It's amazing."

"I think I'll have to," Shelley said with a smile. "Looks like that one's become a real hit at the Cove. They're selling out of it every day."

Margaret wiped her face again. "Okay, so tell me all about it."

Shelley looked at the playground and sighed. "It's Dan. I've been so busy this week that I didn't notice how he was really doing. And he's been trying to put on a good face for my sake."

"Let me guess," Margaret said. "He's becoming depressed because he feels totally useless."

Shelley's face lit up. "That's exactly it. He says he thought I would think he was just being jealous."

"Because of all the big things starting to happen with your baking business, and he's sitting around most of the day doing nothing?"

Shelley nodded. "Turns out he's not jealous at all. He's genuinely happy for me and really hopes the business takes off."

"Good men don't do well with nothing to do," Margaret said. "Especially men like Dan, who are raised with such a strong work ethic."

"Add to that the fact that he's been raised with the idea that men do all the providing. His brothers, his father, grandfather . . . it's always been that way in the Bauer family. I mean, really, that's the reason he got sucked into that scheme with those smugglers. He had to find a way to provide."

"God really spared your family on that one." Margaret kept glancing at the playground as well. She couldn't help but be co-lifeguard.

"He did, and Dan knows that. And he even believes God opened up this door for us at the Cove."

"But none of that helps him," Margaret said.

"No, and the work at the docks seems to be slowly drying up. He said it's just a matter of time before they move from cutting back their hours to handing out pink slips. He's been great around the house. With the kids, I mean, and just helping out in general. But he finished his to-do list of our small projects weeks ago."

Margaret nodded. "I'm so glad Allan found his second wind doing this furniture business. I remember what he was like back when he first retired as a CPA. Three months later, he was miserable. I don't think God means for us to thrive on unending leisure."

"Besides having nothing to do," Shelley continued, "Dan's pretty anxious about the money. We have more hope now that things are beginning to happen with the baking business, but it's going to take a while to start making money, I think." She looked at the metal grille surface of the picnic table. "I just wish there was something else he could do. Something he could do right here in Marble Cove."

Just then, Margaret got an idea.

As soon as it came to her, she immediately wondered why she'd never thought of it before. "Shelley, Dan's great at woodworking, right?"

"Sure. He loved working on Allan's projects last summer. And he's got so many tools in that garage of his that I think he could open a store himself. Why, are you thinking about something else with Allan?"

"No, not exactly. I mean, Allan will have to get involved, at least a little. But we've already talked about Dan helping with his furniture business. Allan just doesn't have enough orders to give him anything steady right now. He did say that if he got a lot of orders off the fall fair this coming week, he might need Dan's help for a few weeks afterward. But I'm thinking of something totally different."

"You mean...like a job, a paying kind of job?"

"Yes, a paying kind of job," she said. "Tell me, has Dan ever built frames for canvases—painting canvases, I mean?"

"I don't think so. Do you mean like fancy gilded picture frames?"

"No, the wood pieces that hold a blank canvas stretched out so someone can paint on it. That's like the skeleton, and the canvas is the skin."

Shelley shook her head. "No, I don't think so. But he's built lots more complex things from wood than that, so I'm sure he could do it. What did you have in mind?"

"I'm hesitant to say until I talk with Allan. But I'm thinking...if I put it all together for him, help him see how it could work, Allan might go for it." She thought a moment. "I really think he would." Ideas started firing off in her mind.

"What is it, Margaret? Can't you tell me?"

"Don't say anything to Dan about this yet, but I'm thinking...if this works out, I might just be able to offer Dan a job myself."

"You mean helping you out down at the gallery?"

"He'd be doing a lot more than just helping me out."

"Margaret...the suspense is killing me. What are you talking about?"

Margaret looked at Shelley. "I'm sorry. I shouldn't have said anything. I really should talk to Allan first. And I'll need a few hours to put all my ideas together on a spreadsheet. That's Allan's world. He's got a great business mind. If I can make it work on a spreadsheet, he'll see it. I just know he will."

"So should I be getting excited?" Shelley asked.

"Not yet," Margaret said. "But start praying. If I'm seeing this right, God might just have a small miracle in store for Dan, like the one he did for you last week. And it will help me, besides."

Chapter Twenty-Three

For the last several hours, Allan had kept coming into the kitchen peeking over Margaret's shoulder, and she'd kept shushing him away. "I don't want you to see it until it's all ready," she'd said. She had been sitting at the kitchen table with her calculator and a scratchpad, working on a proposal. Allan was a businessman. She was writing this proposal to appeal to the businessman in him.

The more she worked on it, the more excited she became. One of his favorite sayings was: "Facts are stubborn things." Well, the facts Margaret was coming up with seemed to be proving her case even more. The proposal was intended to provide support for the great idea that had dawned on her earlier while at the park with Shelley.

Why not hire Dan to build frames for the giclée prints?

She'd priced all the most professional-looking giclée print services she could find online and arrived at the one she wanted to go with. She'd even gotten a sample of their work sent to her—a small canvas print of one of her own photos. Margaret had been thrilled at the detail and vibrancy of the image. It was almost brighter than her original, and it was done with archival inks. She would be proud to let people buy this.

The issue now was the framing. She'd added everything up, and it seemed to her that she could buy the raw materials and pay Dan labor to do the framing and canvas stretching for substantially less than what she'd pay to have the printer do it and then mail the bulkier item to her.

Allan walked into the kitchen once more. "Don't worry, I won't peek. I'm just getting a glass of apple juice." She heard the refrigerator door open. "Am I correct to assume you're hoping to go over that with me tonight?"

"I'm almost finished. Just a few more minutes."

"You see what time it is? My mind is just about finished with this day."

Margaret turned to face him. "See, that's my strategy. To get you when you're totally worn out, so there's no more fight left in you."

Allan walked over to the doorway, holding his glass. "Really, Margaret, what's all this about?"

"It's nothing we haven't talked about already. Just a new way of approaching the solution."

"Is it about this giclée printing idea?"

"Yes. You go on in the living room and finish your apple juice. That's how close I am." He smiled and turned to walk away. "But take nice, slow sips, okay? I'm going to transfer these numbers to a spreadsheet on the computer."

Ten minutes later, she was finished. She got up to call Allan to the office but did so quietly. A few minutes ago, Adelaide had come in to kiss her good night. Margaret sat back in her office chair. Allan walked over and sat in the folding chair they had in the room.

"Come closer," she said. "I need you to see the screen."

"Do I need to get my glasses?"

"You shouldn't. I made the font nice and big, for both our sakes." He scooted his chair closer, and she tilted the screen so they both could see. "I know how you hate being kept in suspense, so I put my big new idea right there in the heading. Go ahead and read it."

He leaned over and read aloud: "'Proposal for Hiring Dan Bauer to Build Wooden Frames for the Giclée Canvas Prints.'" He turned and looked at her. "Wow... didn't see that coming."

"No?"

"I know you'd like to help the Bauers out," Allan said. "We both would. But this...?"

Margaret scrolled the spreadsheet down several inches so he could see what she had worked out. "You look that over a few minutes while I get a glass of water."

When she came back a few minutes later, Allan was doing some calculations of his own. She didn't know if that was a good sign or not, but it did mean he was taking her idea seriously.

She set her glass on the table, walked behind him, and began to massage his neck.

"If I didn't know better, I'd say you're unduly trying to influence me," he said, his face still glued to the screen.

She stopped the massage. "That's not what I'm doing."

"Don't stop. I said 'If I didn't know better.' Actually, I'm pretty impressed with what you put together here."

"So you think it's feasible?"

He tapped his finger on the mouse. "It all depends on you getting the income you're assuming. People will really pay that much for prints?"

"I know it seems like a lot. But yes, they will. The inkjet printer they use puts the exact image of the original right on a blank canvas. I'll sign each print, add a few brush strokes to each one, and make only a limited number. Diane said people treat them like collectibles. From what I've seen on these Web sites, it's really happening. And here..." She held up the clipboard she'd been keeping next to the cash register. "This is a list of customers from the gallery who have already said they want one as soon as I get this thing going."

Allan's left eyebrow rose. "Guaranteed sales, eh? Nice work. But look," he said, pointing to a spot on the screen, "paying Dan as generously as you're suggesting, and doing so now before you're really up and going, will be expensive. Not to mention all the other costs involved in printing and then shipping these canvases. It'll be quite an investment to get started. You're okay with that?"

"It does make me a little nervous," Margaret said. "But take another look at my projected income figures. These are more than just guesses. I went to a number of Web sites to see how much artists are getting for these giclée prints."

Allan looked it over. Slowly, a big smile appeared on his face.

Then on hers.

"Okay, you've convinced me." He turned and looked in her eyes. "You've done a good job here, Margaret."

"Oh, Allan, you really think so?"

"I do. And I think it could really help the Bauers. If you're right about people being willing to pay that much, and if the demand remains high, you'll keep him fairly busy and well paid. You realize, though, that those are some pretty big ifs?"

"I do. But I just know this will work." She got up from her chair and gave him the biggest hug. "So can I tell Shelley about this tomorrow? She'll be so excited."

"Sure, I don't see any reason for us to wait." He patted her back, and she sat down beside him. "In fact," he said, "let's do this the right way. Something like this shouldn't be done in a chat over coffee between you and your friends, especially since it involves Dan. I think he might be more receptive to all this if it came from me. I can see someone like him viewing this as a handout from friends in a time of need. Not like a serious job offer. Why don't you call Shelley and see about having them over to dinner tomorrow night? We'll ask Adelaide to watch the kids while we talk the whole thing over."

"That's a great idea. I really do think it'd be better for Dan to hear all this from you. Maybe I should give Beverly a call too. She's been working on getting a Web site and brochures together for Shelley's baking business. Maybe she can put something together for us too—maybe in time for the fair."

"I don't know how much time she'll have for that this week, but you could start promoting it yourself as much as you can. Of course...all this is assuming Dan says yes. If not, we'll have to revisit this idea. But if he does, get as many names as you can at the fair. Just make sure you tell people it will take a little time to get this printing thing going. I don't want you or Dan biting off more than you can chew."

Margaret didn't know what to say. This had gone so much better than she expected. She couldn't wait to call Shelley tomorrow, couldn't wait to see the look on Dan's face when Allan explained it all.

She just knew he would say yes. How could he say no to something like this?

CHAPTER TWENTY-FOUR

Diane could hardly believe it. She looked down at Rocky, who was sitting by her side, wagging his tail as if he expected her to say something important. "I finished it, Rocky. I finished that all-consuming proposal! Isn't that exciting?" It was Monday, just a few minutes before noon. "And no more tinkering with it—I promise."

He stood up and ran to the door. For him, the proper celebration for anything was a nice walk on the beach.

She laughed. "Okay, buddy."

Diane looked at her computer monitor. When Frieda had called to ask her to do this, it had thrown Diane into a tailspin. But now she was standing there looking at the very thing she had feared, and it was finished and ready to send in. It still made her a little nervous to consider that the entire book deal hinged on whether her agent and publisher shared her enthusiasm. But she had a good feeling about it.

She stood up to get her jacket. "That's all we can do, right, Rocky? Just pray and do our best." He sat by the door vibrating with anticipation, obviously not understanding a word she said. But he knew what it meant when she put on her jacket.

"Oh, I almost forgot." She needed to back up the proposal on her flash drive. Just in case. After the beach walk, she would read the proposal one more time, write an e-mail to her agent, and muster up the courage to hit the send button. "Just one more second, Rocky."

With the file backed up, she opened the front door, and Rocky ran on ahead to the sidewalk. As she closed the door, she noticed Rocky looking the opposite way down the street, toward Beverly's house. He started to bark. She turned to see what had grabbed his attention and saw Beverly and Margaret chatting in front of Beverly's house. Rocky seemed to enjoy the company of her friends almost as much as she did. When she reached the sidewalk, he seemed more interested in going over to visit them than in heading for the beach.

"Okay, boy, you can go." He took off in their direction. She'd been so closed up inside the house this past month that it felt good to be carefree again and to be able to spend unscheduled time with her friends without a nagging sense that she'd better get back to work. Could she make it up to them all for not being there when they'd needed her?

She heard Margaret's voice from down the street. "Rocky, good to see you." Margaret looked in her direction, and so did Beverly. Both waved. "Can you stop and visit a few minutes?" Margaret asked.

"Actually, I finally can." Diane turned down the sidewalk in their direction. "Believe it or not, I just finished my proposal." In a few moments, she had caught up to Rocky. Beverly had bent down and was scratching behind his ears.

"That's wonderful," Margaret said. "Does that mean we get you back now?"

"Yes! I'm going to read it one more time before I send it in, but I think my life will finally start returning to normal."

"You sound upbeat," Beverly said as she stood. "So you're pleased with the end result?"

"I am. Let's just hope my agent and editor feel the same way."

"I'm sure they will," Margaret said. "It will be so great to have you back again."

"You've been as busy as I have this past month, Margaret," Diane said. "I wish I could've helped you more. But I guess now your schedule will start to lighten up?"

"Well, yes and no. In some ways, I think it's about to get even busier. But I'm so excited about it. I was filling Beverly in. You're just in time."

"Great," Diane said. "But Beverly, how's your back or whatever you hurt on the beach the other night? I can't believe you saw the light in the lighthouse!"

Beverly rubbed her lower back. "It's a little stiff, but I'm okay. It was crazy to run out there like that. Even if I hadn't fallen, what would I have done if I'd caught someone?" She laughed.

Diane looked down at Rocky, who had moved next to Margaret. It was her turn to give him some attention. She was glad he was a patient dog, because the beach walk had just been delayed. She couldn't wait to hear all the details. "So, Margaret, what's going on?"

"It's actually your idea, Diane," Margaret said. "It looks like we're going to be able to start the giclée print idea sooner rather than later."

"That's wonderful!" Diane said. "How soon?"

"Maybe right away. I'm arranging for the print service to get digital images of some of my paintings. But first we're having a big meeting with Dan and Shelley to talk this all out. They're coming over to dinner tonight."

Diane was confused. Obviously, she had missed an important detail.

"I'm sorry," Margaret said. "I didn't tell you the best part. Allan and I are going to ask Dan tonight if he'd like to come work for us. Well, for me mostly, doing the framing and canvas stretching these giclée prints will need done so I can display and sell them. I crunched all the numbers and ran the whole thing by Allan last night. He thinks it really could work. Ever since you came up with the idea, the only holdup has been time. Neither of us has had the time to move on it. It never dawned on either one of us to consider getting someone else involved."

"That's great news," Diane said.

"It really is," Margaret said. "I have enough money left over from my advance from the greeting card contract to get started. Even enough to pay Dan for the time it takes him to learn the process. I'll have him building the framework for the canvases, but he's handy enough to even make custom frames to decorate the prints. It occurred to me not long ago that we needed a framer here in Marble Cove. And I've got enough names on my clipboard to start seeing some income flow in right away."

"You'll get a ton more names to add to that clipboard at the fall fair this weekend," Beverly said.

"We hope so," Margaret said.

"Of course you will," Diane said. "This is wonderful. Does Shelley know yet?"

"A little bit. I hated keeping her in suspense, but Allan wants to tell them both tonight. I called her a little while ago to finalize our plans, and she was dying to hear all the details."

"Well," Beverly said, "as I was just telling Margaret, I'm almost done with Shelley's Web site and brochures. Just have a little fine tuning to do. I can't wait for you all to see it. You think you could look over the text parts, Diane? Maybe spice them up a little?"

"I don't see why not," Diane said. "I plan to finish polishing up my proposal this afternoon. After that, I should have plenty of time. Do you want to send me the file or have me come over this evening and look it over?"

"Why don't you come over? The fair starts Friday evening, right?"

"It does," Margaret said. "I can't believe it's so close."

"I was thinking of asking you all over Thursday evening for a dry run," Beverly said. "You know, check out the Web site to make sure everything works."

"I'm happy to say that I can make it," Diane said. Margaret said she could too.

"Great," Beverly said. "I've already asked Shelley, and she can't wait. If you want, Margaret, I could start next week helping you build a Web site to display all your new art prints. Probably won't take me that long after all I learned putting Shelley's together."

"I'd love your help with that," Margaret said.

"Margaret," Diane said, "do you think there's any chance Dan will turn you down?"

"I don't think so," Margaret said. "But Shelley said he's been a little depressed lately. We just need to convince him that we really want him to do this, that it's not some kind of handout. Would you both please pray that God meets us all tonight and everything goes well?"

Just about then, Diane heard Rocky barking several houses down. Apparently, his patience had run out. He ran about ten yards farther, heading toward the beach, then spun around and barked some more.

"As you can see," Diane said, "I've got to go. But I will definitely pray. It won't be hard—I feel like God is really behind all of this. It looks to me like our first miracles in Marble Cove this fall are happening right here, with the Bauer family."

★   ★   ★

The Bauers came over at about six thirty. Allan had thought they should have the meeting at their house. If things didn't go well, it would be a lot easier for the Bauers to find some reason to leave than it would be for them to have to chase Allan and Margaret out of their house. Margaret couldn't imagine things going sour, but she respected Allan's wishes. She had told Shelley that Adelaide could watch the kids in the living room while they talked at the table after dinner.

At the moment, Shelley was with Adelaide getting the kids situated in the living room. Adelaide, of course, was thrilled to spend more time with them. She'd already laid out some toys and all her picture books. Dan was sitting at the table, looking a little bit nervous.

"Allan should be in to join us any second," Margaret said as she poured the coffee. "So how is work going, Dan?"

"Pretty much the way it's been going," he said. "Plenty to do for the first few hours, then it started getting slow. Then they sent us home at lunch. It's really almost become a part-time job now."

"That must be hard." She really didn't know what to say.

"Yeah, it is."

Just then, Allan and Shelley came into the room from different directions. "Sorry to keep you waiting," Allan said as he took his seat. "I hope I didn't miss much."

Margaret brought the coffee cups to the table then back to the counter to fetch the chocolate cream pie. "You are all going to get a chance to taste what the competition will be serving in the bake-off contest this weekend. Mrs. Peabody dropped this off this afternoon. She said she wants to make sure it's just as good as she used to make years ago. Shelley, consider it gathering information about your opponent."

Shelley laughed. "Oh, I've had it before," she said. "I already know how good it tastes."

"I didn't cut it," Margaret said. "So you all take as big a slice as you'd like."

Dan reached over and cut himself a man-sized portion of pie. "So," he said, "Shelley tells me you have some exciting news to share with us."

Margaret sat down and resisted the urge to jump in. She and Allan had talked about letting him lead the conversation.

"We do," Allan said. "But before we get into it, I want you to know, Dan, we don't want you to feel any pressure to say yes to this idea. You don't even have to give us an answer tonight. I expect you and Shelley might want to have some time to talk it over on your own, without the two of us sitting across the table."

"I appreciate that," Dan said. "From the few things Shelley said, sounds like it has something to do with doing some work for you. I've noticed how busy you've been in your workshop lately. Looks like you're getting a lot more orders than before."

"I am. But that's not what this is about."

A surprised look came over Dan's face. "Really?"

"It is about doing some work, but not with my furniture business. Actually, you'd be working more with Margaret, helping her with a new project she'd like to start at the gallery."

"Like what?" Dan said. "Do you need some more painting done?"

"No. We'd like to offer you a job, Dan. And if things go as we're hoping, I think it will be a decent job for you. Margaret has been getting a lot of requests for her art from people who really love her paintings but can't afford to buy an original. We're heading into a new phase of this business. We want to start making custom prints of her paintings available at the gallery, and online too."

Dan's forehead furrowed. "So you need me to do . . . what?"

"We need you to build frames for these canvases," Margaret said, no longer able to contain herself.

"Frames?" Dan's eyes went to the artwork on walls around them. "Like black ones or white ones or fancy ones or whatever?"

Allan shook his head. "No . . . Well, maybe, as part of it. But mainly we'd need you to build the framework—the bones—for the canvases themselves. The boards that keep the canvas stretched out. Then people can put frames on *that* if they wish."

Margaret added, "I am thinking of offering custom framing at the gallery, but that may be a little ways off. You see," Margaret said, "these prints—they're called giclées—will be produced at the print service we'll be using, and they'll send those canvases to us rolled up in tubes. But people can't use that. They can't just tack a canvas on the wall. They need some way to display them. And that's where you'd come in."

Dan looked at Shelley and nodded. "I can build rectangles out of wood . . . sure."

"Well, there's more to it than that," Margaret said. "Sorry, Allan, you go ahead."

Allan smiled at Margaret. "Well, Margaret is the expert, but from what I understand, you have to be very careful not only with building the frame but in stretching the canvas across it. The tension has to be evenly spread or the picture will be skewed, and you can even tear right through it and ruin the print. To be an expert framer is to raise your craftsmanship up to the next level." He gave Dan an evaluating look. "You think you're up to it?"

"You know it."

Margaret loved the way Allan had done this. Now it wasn't a handout—now it was a challenge to excellence. Margaret never would've thought to do it this way.

Dan's posture straightened. "Is there really decent money in this sort of thing? Enough to hire someone?"

"You'd be surprised how much," Allan said. "I certainly was. If things go as we're hoping, this could become your primary source of income, and at least at the same level you've been used to. Of course, we don't know for sure how this will go. Look at it this way, Dan. We're going to have to get these things framed one way or another. People won't buy them in tubes. We either need the printer to frame it, which is amazingly expensive, or need to find someone else to do it. The numbers tell us that, if we can pay you to do these, we can build enough into the sale price for these to give us all a nice profit."

Dan nodded thoughtfully. "Would it be full or part time?"

"Eventually, we see it becoming a full-time job. Margaret and I talked about this. We think you should probably keep your job down at the dock and just work on our framing whenever they let you off early. Between the two, you'd have a full week's work. Then if and when our demand for these got steady, you could give notice at the dock and do this full-time. We can discuss the details later, but I guarantee you'll be making a better hourly rate for us than what they pay you down there."

Dan glanced at Shelley, and Margaret realized Shelley hadn't said a word. But her expression was relaxed, and that had to be a good sign.

"Well, that's the story," Allan said. "You want to take some time to think this over?"

"I don't," Dan said. "I'd love to do this." He looked at Shelley again. She nodded, her eyes wide. "Guess that settles it," he said. "We'll do it."

"That's wonderful!" Margaret said.

Allan reached his hand across the table, and Dan shook it eagerly. Both men stood up, and the wives did the same.

Dan and Shelley put on their jackets and made their way to the side door. As they opened the door, Allan said, "We can work out all the details over the next few days."

"Maybe we should wait until after the fall fair," Margaret said. "Shelley's going to have her hands full between now and then."

Dan turned and looked at Margaret. "I will make you proud of me. I won't let you down. I'm going to... take my craftsmanship to the next level. I'm going to be the greatest canvas framer in the state. Before you know it, we'll have your artwork all over New England. People can have it on greeting cards, and then they can have that same work on their walls."

"Oh no!" Shelley said, suddenly frightened. "The kids!" She ran back into the kitchen. "Where are they?"

"Adelaide!" Margaret called, her heart racing. She'd forgotten all about them.

"Shh." Someone shushed from the direction of the living room.

They all walked into the living room and found the kids asleep. Emma was snoozing on Adelaide's lap, and Aiden was dozing on a pillow at her feet.

"I told them stories," Adelaide said. "I tried to keep them quiet like you said."

"Adelaide, you're an angel!" Shelley said. "You just gave me an amazing gift."

Adelaide's eyes widened. "I did?"

"Trust me. You did."

CHAPTER TWENTY-FIVE

The next three days had been hectic and full, but Diane was having a wonderful time. She had sent in her three-book proposal to Frieda Watley, her literary agent, on Tuesday morning. Then she'd spent all day Tuesday and Wednesday and all of Thursday morning feverishly checking her e-mail and jumping every time her cell phone rang. She was dying to know what Frieda thought of it. If she loved it, Diane could relax. But if she hated it, Diane would have to start over.

To keep her mind occupied, she'd spent most of Tuesday and part of Wednesday going over the text for Shelley's brochures and Web site. Beverly had done a fairly good job, but it did sound much too businesslike. Beverly said she loved the changes Diane had made. Since they'd finished earlier than planned, Beverly had suggested she and Diane work on a surprise project for Margaret.

And so they had.

Diane couldn't wait to spring it on Margaret tonight after the big "reveal" when Beverly showed them Shelley's finished Web site and brochures. Diane was just about to head out the door toward Beverly's to join the other ladies when her cell phone rang.

It was Frieda!

Just answer the phone, she told herself. But she was so nervous. It rang again. She pushed the button. "Hello?"

"Diane, it's Frieda. This a good time?"

"I was just on my way out, but I've got a few minutes."

"That's all I need. Just wanted to get back with you on your proposal."

Diane felt herself tensing up. "So . . . what did you think?"

"I loved it," Frieda said. "It's just what I was hoping for."

"Really?"

"Really, Diane. Oh, I'll do some formatting and tweaking. Have to earn my money, you know. But you did a great job with this. I don't think I'll have any trouble getting this through now."

"Did you have any concerns at all? Any places you felt were a little weak or—"

"No, I didn't. Not really. At this stage of our negotiations, it's just right the way it is. It gets the story across. Once we get down the road a bit, Jane—she's the acquisitions editor for your publisher—might want to tweak a few things. But I'm perfectly happy going forward with this right now."

Diane thought she might cry—or pass out. So much work and so much tension over such a long time. She felt her energy flowing out through her feet. "Well, if you're happy, then I'm happy."

"Great, then I'll get in touch with Jane and get the ball rolling again."

"Thanks, Frieda. And thanks for calling."

"We'll talk soon." She hung up.

Diane was so excited and so relieved. She put her cell phone in her purse, locked the door, and headed down the sidewalk toward Beverly's. She saw Mrs. Peabody standing by her front door enjoying the sunset. Diane waved as she walked by. "It's a beautiful night, isn't it, Mrs. Peabody?"

"It surely is," she said. "I was listening to the weather report on the news just a little while ago. Looks like we'll be having wonderful weather for our fall fair this weekend." She turned to head back inside. "I do hope the judges like my chocolate cream pie this year." She didn't seem to be saying this to Diane, and she had a rather fretful look on her face as she said it.

Diane hoped Mrs. Peabody wasn't setting her heart too strongly on winning this year. Her chocolate cream pie was tasty, and Diane didn't know what Shelley planned to enter into the contest yet. But everything Shelley baked seemed to be in a different league than Mrs. Peabody's chocolate cream pie, as good as it was.

She turned off the main sidewalk onto the flagstone walkway that led up to Beverly's father's front porch. As she tapped the little door knocker, Diane could hear the ladies talking inside.

The door opened. "Hi, Diane, come on in." Beverly's face was bright and happy. "The coffee's ready. We're just sitting around yakking."

They walked down the hallway past the library. Diane looked through the open doorway and saw Beverly's father sitting in his favorite chair watching a baseball game on TV. She followed Beverly into the kitchen, where she saw Shelley and Margaret sitting at the table. Beverly's laptop was on, pushed toward the back of the table so everyone could see.

"Diane," Shelley said, "so glad you could come."

"How are you holding up?" Diane said. "You must be exhausted."

"I know I should be, but I'm not. I guess I'm too excited."

"Hey, Diane, sit over here by me," Margaret said. "We're leaving the middle seat open for Beverly, so she can take us through the Web site."

Diane poured her coffee and sat next to Margaret. "You guys are going to love this. I've already gotten a little preview of what Beverly can do, since I've been working with her the last few days."

"But you haven't seen it online yet," Beverly said. "With everything up and running."

"It's online?" Shelley said. "Already? It's actually online, right now?"

"It's live. I uploaded it late this afternoon," Beverly said. "I wanted to make sure everything worked right before you all came over."

"I have a Web site? My baking business is online right now!"

"You have a Web site," Beverly repeated, smiling. "Your baking business is online right now."

"What if someone goes on there accidentally and places an order?" Margaret asked.

"Don't worry," Beverly said. "The credit card processing piece is offline right now. I tested it, so I know it works, but that part is inactive until you're ready to go."

"But just think," Diane said, "if someone manages to sneak through and place an order while we're taking this guided tour, Shelley will just have to get up and bake them something."

Everyone laughed.

"Are you ready?" Beverly asked.

Shelley nodded.

"Here we go." Beverly typed in Shelley's new Web site address.

A moment later, the site flashed onto the screen. Diane looked at Shelley to catch her reaction. Her eyes grew big and bright, like a child on Christmas morning. "I can't believe it! It's beautiful."

"Look at that," Margaret said. "It's amazing."

To Diane, it looked even more appealing than the pastry cabinet down at the Cove. It put her in mind of a high-end women's magazine. The photos looked professionally done, the colors and overall design were magnificent. It said Martha Stewart and *Better Homes and Gardens* and "I'm smart—you should order from me" all over it.

"This is the home page," Beverly said. "It serves as the anchor for the whole site."

"I wrote that little welcoming paragraph," Diane said, "trying to make it sound like you, Shelley. When you get some time, read it over. If you want to make any changes at all, just let me know. We really want this site to capture your personality, not ours."

"Oh, guys, I don't know what to say. It's too wonderful."

Beverly scrolled down so they could all see the bottom half of the home page. "I thought you could use this section to feature some special dessert you want to draw people's attention to. We can change it out whenever you want to highlight something else. I just decided to put the blueberry crumb cake there for now. That one's become my favorite."

"You're not going to believe this," Shelley said, "but that's the perfect choice to start off with."

"It is?"

"I decided to enter my blueberry crumb cake into the bake-off contest. It's pretty much the same thing I've been making all along, but for the contest I added some extra blueberries and even more butter."

"I think that's an excellent choice." Diane didn't see how Mrs. Peabody could win, even with Shelley's old version.

"Me too," Margaret said.

"I think that decision is going to win you the contest." Beverly moved the cursor to the left side of the page and scrolled back up to the top half. "Over here in this sidebar are all the different categories of desserts. Here, click on any one you want."

For the next few minutes, Shelley clicked on every page. Beverly had set each one up like the dessert menu from a restaurant, with pictures of each dish beside the item's name. When Shelley clicked on the picture, a new page opened with a bigger picture of the dessert and an enticing description detailing the wonderful joys that awaited with every bite. At the bottom of each page was the item's price, with several breakdowns depending on the quantity.

"I don't know if you caught this," Beverly said, "but we decided not to use the language most Web sites use when ordering. They usually say, 'Add to your cart' and have a little icon that looks like a shopping cart. We thought, since this is a bakery . . ." She brought the cursor down to the price section.

"'Add to your box,'" Shelley read aloud.

"And see," Diane said, "Beverly found a little icon that looks like a bakery box."

"That is so *cute*," Shelley said.

"Very clever," Margaret said.

"Well, let's try it," Beverly said. "Shelley, go ahead and order a bunch of things."

She did, and then she followed the prompts as if she'd finished shopping. It immediately went to a page that looked like an invoice.

"When the customer is all done and clicks 'Bake My Order,'" Beverly said, "they'll get an e-mail that looks very much like this invoice."

"What will I get?" Shelley asked. "I'll have to know what to bake and how much and where to send it."

"There's another section of the Web site that's for your eyes only," Beverly said. "Here, I'll type it in." A new page opened, not nearly as fancy, listing all the items Shelley had ordered a few moments ago.

"Would you look at that!" Margaret said.

"You can print out a report," Beverly said, "so you can work without having to be by the computer. Or you can leave the computer on and fill the orders online. But don't worry about the details now. If you're okay with it, I'll leave it offline until after the fair is over."

"Okay with it?" Shelley said. "Beverly, you are a genius!"

It really was quite impressive, Diane thought. It certainly didn't look like a novice Web designer had put this together over a few days.

"I'm so glad you like it," Beverly said. "But don't forget Diane in all this. She was the one who—"

"Now Beverly," Diane said, "don't be modest. I just tweaked the text a little bit. This is your masterpiece."

"Well, both of you, I can't thank you enough," Shelley said. "There are no words..." She got teary, so she just reached over and gave Beverly a big hug. Then she turned around and did the same with Diane.

Beverly stood. "I almost forgot the brochures." She left the kitchen area. When she came back, she was holding a shoebox in her hands. She sat the box on the table and removed the lid.

Shelley pulled some out. "Beverly, these are beautiful! They look just like the Web site."

"That's what I was hoping for," Beverly said. "I had three hundred printed up, but I have no idea if that's enough. It won't be too hard to print more if we need to, maybe by Sunday."

"I love them," Shelley said. "But these must have cost a fortune. You've got to let me pay you for them."

"Nonsense. They cost a lot less than you think, and they're my treat."

Shelley looked through one slowly. "I can't believe it. Here we are on the eve of the fall fair, and all of this has come together like...a miracle." She looked from Beverly and Diane to Margaret. "What you guys have done for Dan and me...it's almost too much to take in. A couple of weeks ago, it seemed like our whole world was falling apart. All we had was the hope that God might do something—and some incredibly good friends to comfort us. I had no idea He would use these same friends to turn everything around. Margaret, you should see what Dan has been like these past few days."

"I was just going to ask you how he was doing," Margaret said.

"He's so happy now," Shelley said. "He's so excited about this new framing thing. Allan told him to do research on framing, and he's paying Dan to do it—enough for us to pay our bills! Dan's already been on the computer several hours over the last few days—and in workshops all over the area—trying to learn everything he can about framing and canvas stretching. He's built several already, and he's constantly talking about it. It's like I have my husband back, Margaret."

"I'm so glad," Margaret said. "I knew God put that idea into my head."

"Should we show Margaret her surprise now?" Diane said to Beverly.

"Seems like the perfect time." Beverly turned and disappeared again, but this time Diane knew where she was going. She came back with another shoebox in her hands, which she set on the table next to Shelley's. "Your turn, Margaret. Open the lid."

"What did you guys do?" Margaret said. She lifted the lid off the box. Then she gasped. "Oh my. Oh my."

"Allan helped us out with this one," Diane said. "He loaded all the digital pictures of your paintings on a jump drive and sneaked them out to us."

Margaret held one of the new brochures in her hands, mouthing the words written across the top, "The Shearwater Gallery." Diane watched her eyes trace each of the paintings as she flipped through the brochure as though unaware that she was looking at her own creations.

"We wanted you to have these to pass out over the weekend," Beverly said.

"We set it up," Diane said, "so that people could take them home and e-mail you if there's a giclée print they'd like to order. It says right there at the end that you'll contact them soon to confirm their order and that you'll let them know as soon as you have the giclée operation up and running."

"We'll get started on your Web site soon," Beverly said. "After things die down from the fall fair."

Margaret sat there, stunned. "I don't know what to say," she finally said. Tears escaped down her cheeks. She wiped her cheeks and looked up. "Of all the things I've experienced and observed living here in Marble Cove, I think one of the greatest miracles is what I've experienced here in this room...the miracle of friendship."

CHAPTER TWENTY-SIX

It was Sunday afternoon. Diane had been splitting her time at the fall fair between helping Shelley just outside the Cove and helping Margaret next door in front of her gallery. Beverly had volunteered to help at both places too. At the moment, Diane was walking back to Margaret's gallery after having stopped by the house to let Rocky out and refill his water bowl.

Diane had always enjoyed the quaint look of the downtown area in Marble Cove, but during the last few days it had been completely transformed. The main streets were all blocked off to traffic. Every shop and restaurant had tables set up out front, offering all kinds of merchandise and food at greatly reduced prices. Lots of free samples and door prizes were being given out all day long. Down the side streets, the craft community was out in full force selling, teaching, and demonstrating techniques to eager fairgoers.

Diane walked by a booth where a line of kids waited to have their faces painted. Across the street, a number of carnival games had been set up. Some she remembered playing as a child, like tossing rings over cartons of soda bottles, trying to throw a football through a hanging tire, and bobbing for apples.

Diane had to step out of the way of a wagon filled with children. It was pulled by what Diane thought appeared to be a very old but patient horse. Mrs. Peabody had been right: the weather throughout the weekend had been splendid.

The fall colors were definitely peaking. She couldn't imagine the leaves becoming any brighter. The yellows were so vibrant in the poplars and elms. The brilliant oranges and reds from the sugar maples and white oaks were astonishing. Lush purples threaded through the scene from the white ash and witch hazels. Everywhere she turned, every scene she saw made her want to get out her camera and click away.

And the crowds were great. She wasn't sure of the exact number, but she'd heard someone say they had over five thousand visitors so far this weekend. They expected even more this afternoon—the final day of the fair—as people came home from church.

She arrived at the gallery, set down her purse, and took a seat behind the table on the sidewalk. She hadn't been there two minutes before a man spoke to her.

"I can take care of things here if you'd like to head next door to Shelley's table for a little while."

Diane looked up. It was Allan, Margaret's husband. "Thanks," Diane said. "It looks like she could use the help. What time is the Chalk Walk Contest?"

"It's at two." Allan looked at his watch. "About an hour from now. Margaret's already over there greeting people and talking with the kids. She's having the time of her life. Lots of people are complimenting her on the painting she's donated for the prize. Of course, I have a feeling that some of them are the parents of kids who entered the contest. It's amusing to see the kind of games people play at a time like this. But they're treating her like a real celebrity, and I couldn't be more proud of her." He took a seat.

"How are things going here?" Diane asked.

"It's been pretty steady," he said. "In fact, we're almost out of the brochures Beverly printed up for Margaret."

"Wow. All three hundred? Do you want me to see if I can get some more printed up to last the rest of the day?"

"I don't think so," Allan said. "Margaret's thinking of closing the gallery at two, when she judges the contest. She cleared it with Maddie Bancroft, the lady in charge of the fair. She sold three originals, which is a great day for her. And have you seen how many names we've added to her list? Every one of them was interested in finding out more about these giclée prints."

"I know. Isn't it wonderful?" Diane said. "It looks like Dan's going to have his hands full once this gets started." Diane stood up and grabbed her purse. "Want me to bring you back something from the Cove?"

"No, thanks," Allan said. "I've got a couple of bottles of Capt'n Eli's Blueberry Pop in the fridge. I'll just grab one of those."

Diane stepped out onto the street and walked around a line of people who'd gathered in front of the Cove. Beverly was handing out free samples of some of Shelley's desserts. A nice breeze started blowing, adding to the pleasantness of the day.

Over to the side, Diane saw Shelley talking with Maddie Bancroft. Shelley looked almost radiant, her countenance bright and cheery. Maddie, on the other hand, looked uncharacteristically worn and frazzled. As she stepped behind the table, she heard the end of their conversation.

"Shelley, everyone is talking about your desserts here at the Cove." Maddie wiped her forehead with a handkerchief. She leaned over and spoke quietly. "I even heard the judges for the bake-off contest talking, about an hour ago. They were raving about your blueberry crumb cake. The announcement of winners is still hours away, so they weren't talking as judges. I'm sure you're a cinch to win that contest."

"Thanks, Maddie," Shelley said. "We sure have been busy here. The traffic at the table has been nonstop the last three days."

"Well, you wouldn't know it by looking at you. I don't know how you manage it all, running the bakery at the Cove, this table out here, your family, and now the new online baking business I read about in your brochure. It looks incredible. I feel exhausted. I might have to soak in the tub for a week just to recover my sanity."

Shelley looked over at Diane and Beverly, then smiled. "I couldn't have pulled this off on my own. What's that song? 'With a Little Help from My Friends.'"

"Well, I better get a move on," Maddie said. "Just stopped by to make sure you'll be sticking around for the bake-off announcement at four. Want to make sure you're there when the judges call your name." Maddie hurried off down Main Street on another errand.

Shelley walked over and stood behind Beverly and Diane. "Well, that's something I never expected to hear… Maddie Bancroft asking me how I manage to get everything done. Thanks so much for stopping by again, Diane. How long can you stay?"

"Almost an hour," Diane said. "I'd like to be there when Margaret announces the winners for the Chalk Walk Contest."

"Oh, I'd like to be there for that too," Beverly said. "But I probably should go check on Father. Is that going to be a problem, Shelley? Leaving you here, stranded?"

"Shouldn't be. Brenna should be back by then. The two of us should be able to manage just fine."

★　　★　　★

It was just a few minutes before two. Diane hurried over to the library, where she found that a large crowd had gathered in a semicircle around the front steps. At the top of the steps, just off the center, she saw Margaret wearing a lovely floral dress and beige sweater. On her right, resting on a wooden easel, stood the painting she had donated for the grand prize winner. On her left stood Maddie Bancroft and a man Diane thought was the principal of the high school. Beside him stood the mayor, members of the town council, and a number of schoolteachers. Most likely art teachers, Diane thought.

Apparently, the Chalk Walk Contest had become a very big deal.

"If I could have your attention, please." It was Maddie, speaking into a mike. "I know you all want to see the great works of art our students have drawn on the sidewalks, but please be careful not to step on them as you gather around. Our special guest judge—the renowned local artist Margaret Hoskins—has taken the time to study all of the creations carefully. She has informed me that she has picked the three winners for each age group and the grand prize winner from among those three. Before I announce the names, I'd like all of the students to line up along the first step here, by age group."

As the crowd moved around to allow the children to find their way to the first step, Diane looked up at her friend Margaret. She was beaming. Diane noticed her wave as she looked over to the crowd on the right. Standing there on the front row were Allan and Adelaide. They smiled and waved back.

"Okay, kids," Maddie said, "I will announce the winners in each category. If you hear your name called, come up here and stand beside me. But before we do that, let's thank Margaret Hoskins for serving as our distinguished judge and for donating this beautiful painting, which will be given to the grand prize winner by Margaret herself."

The crowd erupted into loud applause. No one clapped harder than Adelaide, Allan, or Diane. Over the next few minutes, Maddie called out the names of the three winners, one for each age group. As the winners made their way up the steps, everyone clapped. Additionally, some folks hooted, hollered, and whistled. When the applause subsided, the high school principal stepped up and awarded each winner a nice plaque. He paused between each one, allowing everyone to take pictures, including the photographer from the *Marble Cove Courier*.

The *Courier*'s photographer snapped a group picture of all three winners, the principal, and their proud parents.

"And now," Maddie said, "our judge has said she'd like to take one more look at the three winners to verify her selection of the grand prize winner. I'd like to ask those standing closest to the drawings to back away and give her some room. And if we could keep our conversations to a minimum for the next few moments, that would be great." She turned to Margaret. "Margaret, the concrete is yours."

★   ★   ★

Margaret stepped down to the sidewalk. She stood over the drawing done by the high school winner. It was a colorful depiction of Main Street in the summer. It showed a great deal of promise and, technically, was the best of the three. But, she reminded herself, the young artist was also several years older than her competitors. She'd even included the signs from the various storefronts. Margaret smiled as she read the Shearwater Gallery sign.

Next she walked to the middle school artist's drawing. For her age, it was extraordinary. She'd drawn a lovely winter scene out in the country. A creek, not yet frozen over, ran through the middle. On one side and up a small hill was an old red barn. A tired-looking horse took shelter inside. On the other side of the creek, a wooden fence ran along the edge, weaving in and out through a row of trees.

Margaret walked over to the elementary school winning drawing, which had been done by a young boy. He was so cute that she was tempted to pick him just because of his smile. He'd drawn his best attempt of the Orlean Point lighthouse. His perspectives were off, and the waves along the beach didn't quite look like waves, but it clearly showed the boy had talent. With some help, he could become quite an artist.

But she had made up her mind. She walked back up next to Maddie, trying not to look at the three contestants.

"Have you decided?" Maddie whispered.

"I have."

Maddie took the mike in hand again. "Now, the moment we've all been waiting for has arrived. Margaret, will you come tell us who you've picked as the grand prize winner of the first annual Marble Cove Chalk Walk Contest?"

Margaret took a few steps to her left and Maddie handed her the microphone. "Well, I have to tell you, all of the drawings done by all the finalists were wonderful. I enjoyed looking at each one. It was so hard to pick a winner from any of the categories, let alone one winner from among you all. Some of you have exceptional talent, and I'm not just saying that. That's certainly the case with the three winners

I picked. But after giving it a lot of thought, I've decided that the grand prize winner is . . . Mandy Thompson, representing the middle school age group."

The young girl shouted and jumped up and down. So did her father. He picked her up and twirled her around. As he did, the entire crowd let loose thunderous applause.

Margaret handed the microphone back to Maddie. When the noise quieted down, Maddie said, "Thank you again, Margaret. And congratulations to you, Mandy. I'm sure the photographer would like to get a picture of you and your family beside Margaret's painting. After that, you can take it home with you. It's now yours."

Margaret knew her moment in the spotlight was over, which was just as well. She headed down the steps toward Allan and Adelaide.

But Mandy, the girl who'd won the grand prize, yelled: "Mrs. Hoskins, please don't go. You need to be in the picture with me."

"Oh," Margaret said. "Okay, if you'd like." Now *this* was fun.

CHAPTER TWENTY-SEVEN

After the crowds cleared from around the library, especially from around the "renowned local artist" Margaret Hoskins, Diane went up to congratulate her good friend. Allan and Adelaide were there, and they all talked about how wonderful the day had been. Allan mentioned he'd given out the last of the brochures just before Margaret's big moment.

Beverly called saying she was so sorry she had missed it. She'd gone home to make lunch for her father and make sure he was doing okay, which he was. Mrs. Peabody couldn't be there, of course. She had her hands full getting ready for the bake-off contest. But Beverly planned to be back in time for the announcement of the bake-off finalists, which started at four. Diane had to go home for a little while to let Rocky out.

Margaret, Diane, and Beverly had agreed to rendezvous in front of the Cove ten minutes before the final bake-off judging began.

At the appointed time, Diane navigated her way through the crowds of happy locals and tourists. She spotted Beverly and Margaret right where they were supposed to be. Brenna sat behind the table watching over the last remnants of all that Shelley had baked for the event.

When Diane caught the eye of Beverly and Margaret, she waved. Already, large numbers of people had begun to funnel down the street to where the bake-off contest was being held. "We better get a move on," Diane said to her two friends, "or we won't get a good spot."

"You two go on ahead," Margaret said. "I'm afraid these stubby little legs and these dress shoes are going to slow me down. I should have asked Allan to bring something more comfortable for my feet for after the contest."

"Don't worry, Margaret. You're doing fine," Beverly said as they walked. "Is this pace okay for you?"

Margaret nodded. "For this distance, I think so."

To Diane, the crowd for the bake-off contest seemed almost double the size of the turnout for the Chalk Walk Contest. "Why do you think there are so many people?"

"Probably because it's the last big organized event of the week," Beverly said.

"I'm sure that's partly why," Margaret said. "But this contest is also pretty old. They've been doing it every year since the fall fair began. Mainers do love their desserts."

Diane looked over the heads of the gathering crowd toward the center table. She couldn't see the desserts, but she knew from something Shelley had explained earlier, that just prior to the moment the judges announced the winner, they laid out on that table their selections for the finalists. Then they let Maddie Bancroft know who the finalists were, and she was to make sure the finalists were present when the winner was proclaimed.

"I see Shelley," Beverly said. "See her? She's one of the finalists. She's standing behind the finalists' table."

Diane saw her too. "Of course she's with the finalists! This is so exciting."

"I can't see over everybody's head," Margaret said. "If I were younger, I'd ask one of you ladies to pick me up."

They laughed.

They really were pretty far back, Diane thought. There had to be something she could do. "Wait a minute," she said. "If the two of you don't mind watching this from an odd angle, I see a spot open in the front, but it's on the far left."

"Lead the way," Margaret said.

Diane carefully steered them around the outer fringes of the crowd until they approached the far left side. She looked behind her and saw Margaret and Beverly a few steps away. "How are we doing?"

"We're right behind you," Margaret said. "You're doing fine."

Sure enough, when she reached the front, the crowd thinned out, and the ladies were able to line up on the first row. Shelley noticed them, smiled, and waved. Diane wondered why people tended to avoid the side sections in big events, preferring to remain in the center areas, even if it meant they had a lousy view way in the back. Then she remembered why she had even thought of this in the first place. It was Eric. Her darling Eric.

Eric had noticed this "phenomenon," as he called it, many years ago, back when they had first begun dating. Whether it was an event like this, a concert, or any other event that didn't use assigned seating, he said you could always find great seats near the front if you didn't mind watching people's profiles. She didn't, and so he'd led her to spots like this much the way she had just led Margaret and Beverly, more times than she could count over the years.

She was so glad she could recall this sweet memory of him without being overtaken with grief and sadness. She released a contented sigh.

"Uh-oh," Margaret whispered. "Do you see who's standing on the other side of Maddie Bancroft?"

"Well, what do you know?" Beverly said. "Good for her."

Diane looked. It was Mrs. Peabody. "Guess she's a finalist too." She looked at the table in front of Mrs. Peabody and saw her familiar chocolate cream pie. Three other women stood behind the table, but Diane didn't recognize them. "I don't understand something," she said to Margaret. "None of the five finalists' dessert dishes have any missing pieces."

"That's a little tradition they started years ago," Margaret said. "They ask everyone who enters to make a second dish of their entry, in case they became finalists. It's kind of a big honor when the judge asks you to bring your second dish to the finalists' table."

"I think it adds to the drama," Beverly said. "Watch—in a moment, they'll walk slowly back and forth in front of the tables. And the crowd will get real quiet."

Diane turned back to watch, and that's exactly what happened. There were three judges, two men and a woman. She recognized the woman as the mayor, Evelyn Waters.

For what seemed like several minutes, the judges continued to pace back and forth in front of the finalists' table. They pointed at different dishes and whispered things to one another. Diane studied their eyes closely. She was sure she saw all three of them eyeing Shelley's blueberry crumb cake far more often than all the others.

Finally, the mayor walked up to the mike. "We want to taste fresh samples of three dishes." The crowd began to buzz. "Could we each have a small slice of...the red velvet whoopie pie, the blueberry crumb cake, and the chocolate cream pie?" The crowd erupted with applause, knowing that the five finalists had now been narrowed down to three.

"Shelley's going to win it. I just know it," Beverly said quietly.

"I agree," Margaret said. "Did you see their eyes when they were whispering? All three of them were looking right at her dish. They're just going through the motions now to build suspense."

Maddie Bancroft brought out three china plates and set them on the table. Every eye was on her as she cut three slices from each dish and set them on the plates. The mayor whispered something to her that caused her to laugh. She walked over to the microphone and said, "The mayor has just informed me that my sample slices were entirely too small." The crowd laughed.

No one spoke for a few minutes as the judges took one bite after another.

After a few minutes, Mayor Evelyn Waters walked up to the mike. "We have narrowed our decision down to two possible winners," she said. "The third-place ribbon will go to the red velvet whoopie pie. Which means that the bake-off contest winner will be either...someone we all know, a woman who has won this contest several times in previous years. Or"—she turned and looked at Shelley—"someone who has entered this competition for the first time." Mild applause followed. "But, of course, we will need to eat a few more bites from each of these final two dishes just to be sure."

The crowd became quiet again. Diane watched the judges' faces as they ate. It was abundantly clear to her that all three judges had much bigger reactions after eating Shelley's blueberry crumb cake than when they tasted Mrs. Peabody's chocolate cream pie. Diane quickly glanced at Shelley, wondering if she noticed it too. It seemed she did, like she was trying to restrain a smile.

The judges took a few more bites from each dish then talked some more. The crowd was silent.

Diane saw them nodding, then all three walked to the microphone, the mayor standing in front. "We have reached our decision," she said. "It was very close, but we have selected a winner. Before I announce her name, I am claiming a prize for myself, my reward for all the hard work I do as your mayor." The crowd laughed. "I get to bring home whatever is left of both of these dishes."

The crowd laughed again, and someone yelled out, "For Pete's sake, May-ah, tell us who won!" The crowd laughed even harder. Some of them clapped.

Diane looked at the two women. Ms. Peabody's face seemed a little tense. Shelley was smiling.

"The winner for this year's annual bake-off contest is...Shelley Bauer and her blueberry crumb cake!"

Everyone cheered and clapped. Even Mrs. Peabody. She moved off to the side to allow Shelley to own the spotlight.

"How wonderful," Margaret said.

Diane looked at Mrs. Peabody's face. She looked disappointed but not crushed. The crowd continued to cheer as Maddie Bancroft handed the mayor the big blue ribbon, and the mayor handed it to Shelley. Shelley took it and waved it before the crowd, eliciting another round of applause. Shelley bent down and gave Mrs. Peabody a gentle hug.

After a few moments, Maddie stepped up to the microphone. "Before you all disperse, I have one final big announcement. Those of you who've been here in past years are used to the bake-off contest being the last event of our fall fair. But this year, we have a big surprise for you. It will take place just after dark, so there's plenty of time to walk around and see some things you haven't seen or see some things again. All the restaurants and eateries know about this, so they've arranged to have extra food on hand if you'd like to grab a bite to eat first."

"You gonna tell us what it is?" someone yelled.

"I am. We'll be showing *The Wizard of Oz*. It will be down the street here, projected right on the big white wall just on the other side of the post office. It'll be like an old time drive-in theater."

The crowd cheered.

"The weather's supposed to stay nice all evening. We can use that big empty field beside it. I thought everyone could set blankets down or bring fold-up chairs. The best part is... it's free. The only thing we ask is for everyone to pick up after themselves when they're done. So, grab a bite to eat and come back later for our big movie. We should be ready about seven."

The crowd began to break up. Diane saw Shelley walk toward her friends. From somewhere in the middle of the crowd, Dan emerged holding Aiden's hand and pushing Emma in the stroller. When he saw his mother, Aiden broke free and ran to greet her. She picked him up and gave him a hug.

"I saw you, Mommy! All those people were talking about your cake."

"They were," she said.

"Did you win the prize?"

"Yes, I did," she said.

Dan walked up, just as Diane, Beverly, and Margaret reached her. "I'm so proud of you, Shelley. Mrs. Peabody's pie is good, but I never had a doubt who'd win."

"Well, I wasn't sure," she said. "Until right at the end, when I looked at the judges' faces."

"We're so happy for you, Shelley," Beverly said.

"Hey, how did things end up at the Cove?" Shelley asked.

"I saw Brenna when I came back after getting lunch for Father," Beverly said. "There was hardly anything left on the table or in the pastry cabinet. I'm sure every last pastry is gone by now."

Just then, Allan and Adelaide walked up and congratulated Shelley. "So what do you think?" Allan said. "About the movie, I mean. Adelaide and I'd like to see it."

"It sounds like fun," Dan said, "but I'm pooped. And the kids are too."

"Not to mention they'd be scared to death," Shelley said. "I had nightmares as a kid the first time I saw it. That wicked witch, all green, and that screechy voice…*I'll get you, my pretty.*"

"The flying monkeys scare me a little," Adelaide confessed.

"I'm definitely wiped out," Beverly said.

"Me too," Diane said.

"I think I'm too tired to join you, Allan," Margaret said. "But I don't mind if you two want to go."

"Well, you want to grab something to eat first?" Allan asked. "You folks gotta eat, right?"

"Dan," Shelley said, "why don't you take the kids back to the house? I'd like to hang out here a while if that's all right."

"Are you kidding? You're the big winner. Stay here and be a celebrity for a change."

They hugged, and Shelley kissed the kids. Then Dan headed out with them.

"So, where should we eat?" Shelley said.

As they began to discuss it, out of the corner of her eye, Diane noticed someone waving. She turned and saw August Jackson by the curb on the other side of the street. He was definitely waving at her.

"Excuse me," Diane said. "I'll be right back." She walked across the street.

"I saw him," August said. "He was here at the fair this afternoon."

"You saw who, Augie?"

"Your mystery man. You know: the tall, dark stranger. The guy who's been coming around asking about the lighthouse."

"He's here...now?"

"I saw him not ten minutes ago."

Chapter Twenty-Eight

Diane brought her friends over to Augie. "Did you talk to him?"

"Didn't get a chance to," Augie replied. "By the time I got to where he was, I'd lost him in the crowd. I was planning to tell him you all were looking for him. After I lost him, I started looking for one of you ladies."

"Augie," Diane said, "would you stay right here for a minute?"

"Sure, I'm in no hurry."

Diane took the others aside. "What do we want to do about this?"

"I wonder if he's here right now," Shelley said, looking around. "Maybe we can talk to him."

"Oh, this is so exciting," Margaret said. "That would be a wonderful way to top off a wonderful day, wouldn't it? Solving this riddle that's been eluding us, for what, almost a month now."

"What are you all going on about?" Allan asked, joining their huddle.

"You remember, hon," Margaret said, "that young man we've been trying to find, the one who keeps coming into town, asking all those questions about the history of the lighthouse."

"I do remember you saying something about it," Allan said. "And do you remember what I said then?"

"You thought it was a silly thing for a bunch of grown women to be fiddling with."

"Oh, Allan," Diane said, "you know how we love a good mystery."

"I do. And I guess, with you being a mystery writer, a thing like this is right up your alley," he said, smiling. He looked at Margaret. "I suppose you're going to want to skip out on eating with me and Adelaide and run off after this thing."

"Do you mind?" Margaret said. "It's just...we might not get another chance to sort this out. The man's in town...right this moment."

"Right this moment?" Allan said. "So you're going to skip dinner altogether?"

"No, we'll get something to eat later. We don't know how long he's going to be in town."

"I suppose a husband should be concerned when he hears his wife's running all over town searching for a younger man."

"You have nothing to worry about," Margaret said.

"Well, you ladies go on then. Adelaide and I will be just fine."

"You sure you don't mind?" Margaret said.

"I don't mind. You're sure it's safe?"

"I'm sure," Margaret said.

"I'm sure he's harmless," Diane added. "Augie's talked with him several times and so has Abby over at the *Courier*. They both said he was very nice."

"Then I guess I better let you get to it, before the trail gets cold." He gave Margaret a hug. She hugged Adelaide too, and the friends hurried over to talk with August Jackson again.

"So...Augie," Beverly said, "when did you see him last?"

"Maybe fifteen minutes ago, twenty at the most. He was standing here on the fringe of the crowd watching the bake-off contest."

"Did you see which way he went?" Margaret asked.

"Maybe...at least I thought it was him. But folks were going every which way after the crowd started breaking up. But since I knew you all were keen on finding him, I tried to keep him in my sights. Thought I saw him heading toward the beach, but I can't swear it was him. By the time I got to where he'd been, he was over a block away, and I just saw him from the back. But I'm pretty sure it was him."

"Do you think he might be heading for the lighthouse?" Diane asked.

"Can't be sure," Augie said. "But that would make sense."

"Or," Shelley said, "it could be he just parked his car on that section of the road."

"If that's the case, he'll be long gone by now," Margaret said.

For a few moments, they all just stood there. "So what do you think?" Diane asked her friends. "Do we go after him?"

"Aw," Augie said, "go on. What have you got to lose? No one's going to think any worse of you than they already do."

"Augie," Diane said, but she instantly saw a smile on his face.

"Nobody thinks you're nuts," he said. "Except Gerald and me, but we haven't said anything to anyone else."

"I think my husband's inclined to agree with you," Margaret said.

"I'm pretty sure Detective Little's in that club too," Shelley said. "Speaking of Detective Little, maybe we should get him involved here before we go heading up to the lighthouse. Just in case there is any trouble."

"You think there could be?" Margaret said.

"I don't mean trouble as in danger," Shelley said. "But you know how concerned he's been about us and this whole lighthouse thing."

"Well, listen, ladies," Augie said, "I'm going to let you figure out your next step while I get some dinner. If you solve this mystery, one of you be sure and let me know."

"We will, Augie," Diane said. "And thanks for coming to tell me about this."

"Happy to oblige," he said as he headed down the sidewalk.

Diane turned to face her friends. "I do think we should get Detective Little involved, but maybe we should wait until we actually have something for him to see. We don't even know if this guy went to the lighthouse."

"Good idea," Margaret said. "How about we head down to the beach and get to where we can see the lighthouse more clearly? If we see anything suspicious, two of us can go get him while the others keep an eye on the lighthouse." She looked up at the sun, which had now fully set.

Beverly hadn't weighed in on this yet. Diane looked at her. If she read the look on Beverly's face correctly, she wasn't quite agreeing with what everyone was saying. "What do you think, Beverly?"

"I understand the concern about involving Detective Little, but I don't want to get our mysterious stranger in trouble if he isn't doing anything wrong. And it doesn't sound like he is. I mean, I think we're all wondering the same thing...this guy is probably the one getting inside the lighthouse, the source of all those mysterious lights we've been seeing these past few months. But he might just be looking for some answers, like we are. If we get Detective Little involved right now...what if he arrests this guy for trespassing because of us?"

The others nodded. No one wanted that.

"You know," Margaret said. "I think we're getting ahead of ourselves here. We don't even know if this fellow is still in town, let alone at the lighthouse. Why don't we take it one step at a time? Let's head over there and see what the situation is."

They all agreed and started walking toward the wooden boardwalk deck. As soon as they cleared the last of the buildings nearest to the beach, the lighthouse came into view.

They looked up and noticed the same thing—there were no lights on, at the top or around the base of the structure.

"Well, it's still not completely dark out," Shelley said. "He might still be over there. It's just that he can see well enough and doesn't need a light."

"I don't know," Beverly said. "It looks pretty covered in shadows. And remember how dark it is inside?"

"I've got two flashlights at the gallery," Margaret said. "We could stop by and pick them up."

Beverly sighed. "All right, but let's agree that if we don't see any lights on at the lighthouse when we get there, we'll just forget about this lighthouse mystery thing."

"What?" Shelley said. "You mean...forever?"

"No." Beverly smiled. "I mean for tonight."

"How about Margaret and I get those flashlights," Diane said, "and we'll meet you down where the boardwalk is closest to the beach? You two keep an eye out and call my cell phone if you see anything new."

They agreed.

It took Margaret and Diane about fifteen minutes to get the flashlights and rejoin their friends. When they walked up to them, they were staring down the beach toward the lighthouse. The last sliver of daylight was quickly fading from the western sky.

Suddenly Beverly shouted and pointed toward the lighthouse. "Do you see that? There's someone, a man, walking down by the foundation."

Everyone looked.

"I don't see anyone," Margaret said.

"Me either," Diane said.

"There he is, just above the rocks. See him?"

"I see him," Shelley said. "C'mon, let's follow him. If we run, I think we can catch him before he goes inside."

"You three run on ahead," Margaret said. "I'll walk as fast as I can."

"I'll stay here with you," Diane said.

"No one should be running," Beverly said. "Or don't you remember my fall the other day? If we have to keep our flashlights off, we should *not* be running."

"C'mon, Beverly." Shelley quickly climbed down to the sand, with Beverly right behind her. "We won't run, but surely a little speed walking wouldn't hurt anything." A moment later, they were all but trotting down the beach.

Soon, Margaret and Diane made their way down. Diane looked ahead, keeping her eye on Shelley and Beverly. She looked beyond them to the lighthouse, but she couldn't see a soul moving about.

"Isn't this exciting?" Margaret said.

"I love it," Diane said. "I wonder who he is and what he's up to."

Margaret looked toward the top of the lighthouse. "Maybe tonight we'll solve our lighthouse mystery once and for all."

Suddenly, a light pierced the lighthouse windows. Not a small light, as though someone held a flashlight or lantern. It was the big light! Not only was it on, but it began to move.

Diane and Margaret stopped in awe as it cut a wide arc out across the water. "What in the world?" Margaret said.

"C'mon, Beverly!" It was Shelley. They had seen it too. Their trotting turned into a run.

Margaret and Diane picked up their pace as fast as they could. As they approached the base of the property, they saw Shelley and Beverly waiting for them. The light was off now.

After she caught her breath, Beverly said, "I thought maybe we should wait for you. There's strength in numbers, and it's pretty dark to be walking up there now."

Diane looked down. That's right: she and Margaret were holding the flashlights.

"Looks kind of spooky," Shelley said. "Did you all see the big light come on?"

They all nodded. What in the world was going on? Diane wondered.

As they approached the lighthouse, Margaret handed Beverly her flashlight. "You should have this, Beverly. Despite recent evidence to the contrary, you're still a lot more sure-footed than I am. You lead the way."

The three of them walked carefully behind Beverly. Diane did her best to keep the flashlight on the ground by their feet a few steps ahead.

When they reached the heavy wooden door, Beverly wrestled with the knob. It was locked. She banged hard on it a few times, but there was no response. Diane didn't expect there would be. This mysterious man appeared to be somewhere near the top of the lighthouse. What else could explain the big light suddenly turning on?

Beverly backed a step away from the door. The others stood behind her, puzzling what to do next.

"Maybe we should head back," Margaret suggested.

"Maybe you're right," Diane said. She wasn't feeling all that confident about solving this mystery just now.

They were about to give up when they heard what sounded like footsteps coming from the other side of the door. Suddenly, the massive door creaked open.

They stood there in stunned silence as a tall man stepped out. Without thinking, both Diane and Beverly shined their flashlights in his face. He was handsome, and he appeared to be in his mid-forties. He reached up and shielded his eyes.

"Sorry," Diane said, lowering hers slightly. Beverly did the same.

By the look on the man's face, it was obvious that he was as shocked to see them as they were to see him. But when he realized he was surrounded by four trembling women, he quickly recovered. He smiled and in a deep voice, said, "Hello there, ladies."

His voice and his smile soon put them at ease. Diane smiled as she realized that he was actually all three: tall, dark, *and* handsome. She looked at Margaret and Shelley. The fear was gone from their faces, as well.

But then she looked at Beverly.

Beverly looked as if she'd just seen a sea monster. She was actually shaking. Her gaze was fixed on the handsome stranger. But the look in her eyes...

The man's eyes grew wide as he noticed Beverly. "Anna?" he said. "Is that really you?"

Diane looked at Beverly and then back at the man. "Look, mister, no one here is named Anna." She looked at her friends for their affirmation.

Margaret and Shelley shook their heads. "You must be thinking of someone else," Margaret said.

Beverly's eyes were cast downward.

The man bowed his head to get a better look at Beverly. "Anna, it *is* you. I can't believe it."

Author Bio

Autumn Light is Dan Walsh's sixth novel and his first for Guideposts. He retired from pastoral ministry in 2010 to write full time, after serving twenty-five years in the same church. Dan would describe himself more as a writer who became a pastor than as a pastor who became a writer. He's wanted to write novels since he was in high school, before he sensed a call to ministry. He's grateful God has given him the opportunity now to enjoy this lifelong dream. His first novel, *The Unfinished Gift*, won two ACFW Book-of-the-Year awards. You can find out more about Dan at danwalshbooks.com. He's been married to Cindi, the love of his life, for thirty-five years. He credits her friendship and insights for helping his books to be so appealing to female readers. Cindi and Dan have two married children and two grandchildren. They live in the Daytona Beach, Florida, area.

A CONVERSATION WITH
DAN WALSH

Q. What was your favorite scene to write in Autumn Light?

A. I think it might be the scene at the Cove where Diane suddenly gets an idea that might solve her friend Shelley's big dilemma. Everything changes after that (but I can't say more, lest I give it away).

Q. What parts of Autumn Light *and* Marble Cove *do you relate to most personally?*

A. My book starts at the beginning of the autumn season, which also happens to be the season of life we are entering now. I also *love* the pace of life in Marble Cove, and my wife and I live in a beach town (like Diane, walking on the beach is one of our favorite pastimes).

Q. The series is called Miracles of Marble Cove. *What miraculous event(s) have you witnessed or experienced in your life?*

A. I've been a Christian since 1975; I've seen more miraculous events than I can number. Among them would be my daughter's palsied hand being completely restored and my son's full recovery from life-dominating asthma (this just happened this past year).

Q. *Who is your favorite character in* Autumn Light, *and why?*

A. It would have to be Diane. I'm amazed at her strength, after losing her husband so young. My sister lost her husband at age forty-five (he was also my best friend; she reminds me a little of Diane). I love the way Diane is so focused on helping her friends, even when her own life is filled with deadlines and pressure.

Q. *What advice would you give to Marble Cove's new novelist, Diane?*

A. Diane: keep fueling your love of writing by feeding your love of reading. Read good books. Read them first as a reader, then go back and read them as a writer, trying to understand what makes them work so well. Read good books about writing and—this is very important—get comfortable listening to input and advice.

Q. *When did you know you wanted to be a writer?*

A. At the end of my eleventh grade Composition class after my teacher, Mrs. Longnecker, took me aside and said, "You really have a gift. You could be a writer if you wanted to."

Q. What is your writing process?

A. I start each day with a lengthy quiet time (prayer and reading). Then take care of all my e-mails and administrative tasks, otherwise they keep nagging me while I'm writing. That leaves the better part of my day to just write, which I usually do for the next four to six hours.

Q. You were a pastor before you became a writer. How do the two occupations compare? What aspects of being a pastor carry over into being a writer?

A. They are similar in that both involve long periods of solitude, and both involve study and a lot of writing (my average sermon was over six thousand words each week). The biggest difference? My telephone rang constantly as a pastor, now it hardly ever does (and I love that). I'm not sure how much carries over from one to the other, except perhaps that being a pastor has helped me to listen to people's hearts, not just their words (that can only help the characters I create for my books).

Q. What would you like your readers to take away from your books?

A. I want them to be thoroughly entertained but also inspired to keep looking to the One who is able to work all things together for good. And also, to ponder the things in life that matter most.

Baking with Shelley

Augie's Blueberry-Almond Muffins

2 cups all-purpose flour
⅔ cup sugar
1 tablespoon baking powder
½ teaspoon baking soda
¼ teaspoon salt
¼ cup vegetable oil
1 egg
1 cup milk
½ tablespoon vanilla
½ tablespoon almond extract
1 cup fresh or frozen blueberries

Preheat oven to 350 degrees. In medium bowl, whisk together flour, sugar, baking powder, baking soda, and salt. In another bowl combine oil, egg, milk, vanilla, and almond extract until well blended. Pour liquid mixture into dry ingredients and stir until not quite all combined.

Add blueberries and gently finish mixing. Spoon batter into eighteen muffin cups, filling each about two thirds full. Bake about fifteen to eighteen minutes, until a toothpick inserted in the center comes out clean.

From the
Guideposts Archives

This story by Diana M. Amadeo of Merrimack,
New Hampshire, originally appeared in
the November 2006 issue of *Guideposts*.

Desiree, my six-year-old daughter, kicked the autumn leaves along the sidewalk into a neat pile as we walked to the school bus that morning. I should have accompanied her in my wheelchair, but opted for my crutches instead. I have multiple sclerosis, and my neuropathy was acting up. Still, like Desiree, I loved the satisfying crunch of leaves underfoot. Autumn is magical here in New Hampshire. I can't think of any sight more breathtaking than the mountains cloaked in the blazing yellows, fiery reds, and burnished golds of the birch, oak, and maple leaves.

My daughter skipped along in the crisp air. I tried to keep pace, but couldn't. I didn't want her to see how much pain I was in. She bent down, scooped up an armful of leaves and sent them flying into the air. They cascaded down around us, and Desiree giggled. "Brown, yellow, orange, green! Red is my favorite. Is it yours too, Mommy?" Her smile faded as she looked into my eyes. "Mommy, are you okay?" She reached out to hug me.

I embraced my baby as best I could. "Your hugs always make me feel better," I said. It was true: For the first time that morning, I had a brief respite from the pain.

But as soon as we got to the school-bus stop, the spasms resumed. I need to go home and take some pain medication, I told myself. I wouldn't be able to wait much longer. The pain was intense, like thousands of sharp, thin needles piercing my legs. Desiree played in the leaves. I paced, groaned and prayed for relief. Where is that bus?

I forced myself forward, wondering how I would make it back to the house when my whole body was in spasm. Then I felt myself lurch to one side. I nearly toppled. Damp leaves had attached themselves to the rubber tips of my crutches, making them slick and dangerous. I picked up one crutch and shook the leaves free. Then I stabilized myself against the clean one so I could shake the leaves off the other crutch. They all fell off except one. The leaf stubbornly held on.

"I'll get it," Desiree said. She knelt down and pulled the offending leaf off the crutch. "Mommy, look!" she gasped.

In her hand was a bright crimson maple leaf. Around its center vein was a perfectly shaped, unmistakable heart. The school bus's brakes screeched. Flashing me a big smile, Desiree handed me the leaf. I bent down and gave her a kiss, then she waved good-bye and got on the bus.

I gingerly held on to the crimson leaf with the perfectly shaped heart as though it were fine porcelain. I hardly remember walking home. I often wonder if I floated back. All I can recall is feeling totally enveloped in God's love, and in awe of the beauty all around me.

That afternoon I met Desiree at the bus stop. I had the leaf with me. "I have an idea," I told her. "I never want to forget this wonderful day. Let's go have the leaf laminated at the copy shop so we can keep it forever."

Desiree is in high school now, and my MS is in remission. And the maple leaf? It still hangs on the glass door of our breakfast nook, its perfect heart a reminder of that perfect autumn day, and of God's restorative promise—bright, beautiful, holy.

Read on for a sneak peak of the next exciting book in
Miracles of Marble Cove!

Still Waters
by Melody Carlson

Shelley looked at the handsome man standing in the doorway of the lighthouse. Who was he? And how had he gotten in?

She and her three friends—Beverly, Diane, and Margaret—had heard that the mysterious man who'd been asking about the lighthouse was in town and might be at the lighthouse itself. Then, as they'd headed this way, the lighthouse beam had come on. After generations of darkness, it was on! And now they stood here confronting the stranger.

But he had eyes only for Beverly.

"Anna?" The man's dark eyes grew wide as he stared directly at Beverly. "Is that really you?"

"Look, mister," Diane said, "no one here is named Anna."

"You must be thinking of someone else," Margaret said.

The man bowed his head to get a better look at Beverly. "Anna, it *is* you. I can't believe it."

The five of them stood there in shocked silence. Shelley thought Beverly looked more embarrassed than shocked, though.

"Excuse me," Diane said, "but this is *Beverly.*" Then Diane proceeded to introduce all the women to the handsome stranger. Shelley thought it seemed slightly absurd, as if they'd casually gathered at the lighthouse for a Tupperware party. They shouldn't be sharing any details with this stranger, even if he did look a bit like a younger George Clooney.

"Nice to meet you all," the man said, finally tearing his eyes from Beverly. "My name is Jeff Mackenzie, and I'm doing research on the lighthouse."

"But at night?" Margaret asked.

"I just wanted to try something when it was dark," he told them. "Kind of an experiment."

"So you were the one making the light work?" Diane asked.

He chuckled. "Yes. I hope it didn't bother you."

"We figured there was a logical explanation," Margaret said.

It was funny now, as if everyone was relaxed and enjoying the moment. Except for Beverly. She still seemed upset. Shelley wasn't sure why, but something was definitely wrong.

"You girls go on and head home without me," Beverly suddenly told them. Her expression was hard to read. "Mr. Mackenzie is an old acquaintance of mine, and I really need to speak to him privately." And with no further explanation, Beverly stepped away from her friends, then followed this strikingly handsome stranger straight into the lighthouse. Just like that, she left Diane, Margaret, and

Shelley standing on the other side as the heavy door closed with a solid-sounding thud.

"What is going on?" Shelley demanded. "Why did she go in there with him?"

"It seems that Beverly already knows Mr. Mackenzie." Margaret sounded aggravatingly nonchalant, as if it was of no concern that Beverly had gone in there with him.

"Apparently they want to be alone," Diane said wryly.

Margaret chuckled. "Can't blame her for wanting to get reacquainted. He's an awfully good-looking man."

"But I don't get it," Shelley said. "At first she seemed so scared. Then she goes off with him. And why did he call her 'Anna'?"

"I'm sure we'll find out soon enough," Diane said. "In the meantime, I'm tired. And I left Rocky home alone."

Margaret hooked her arm in Shelley's. "Remember what curiosity did to the cat, Shelley. Better get you home." She turned her flashlight beam back toward the beach, and the three of them slowly headed back toward town.

Naturally Shelley continued to ponder the strange occurrence, trying to get her friends to speculate with her. But the fact was that no one really knew what was going on. As mysterious as this Jeff Mackenzie had seemed initially, Beverly's reaction seemed even more mysterious. Perhaps they didn't know her as well as they supposed.

A NOTE FROM THE EDITORS

Miracles of Marble Cove was created by the Books and Inspirational Media Division of Guideposts, a nonprofit organization that touches millions of lives every day through products and services that inspire, encourage and uplift. Our magazines, books, prayer network (OurPrayer. org), and other outreach programs help people connect their faith-filled values to daily life.

Your purchase of *Miracles of Marble Cove* makes a difference. When you buy Guideposts products, you're helping fund our work, which includes ministry to military personnel, prisons, hospitals, nursing homes and educational institutions. To learn more, visit GuidepostsFoundation.org.

To find out about our other publications and to enjoy free online resources such as inspirational newsletters, blogs, videos, Facebook and Twitter links, visit us at Guideposts.org.